UNDER THE LONESOME SKY

Thomas McNulty

WOUNDED
OUTLAW
BOOKS
2023

Dedicated to my beautiful wife Jan!

CONTENTS

Chapter 1

He dreamed about Atlanta burning.

In his dream General Sherman rode past him on a black horse, his eyes blazing with intensity. Sherman was craggy but regal and truly a man to admire. But the sky was black and the air was alive with black locusts. He wanted to see the stars again but the heavens were blotted by artillery smoke. His world was black and thundering with canon and the endless popping of the Springfield rifles. "Damn your eyes to hell!" A man screamed as he raised his Navy Colt and shot him through the head. His world was a battle song composed of hunger, fear, pain and the screams of the wounded. The sound slithered in the air, poised like a rattlesnake, its tail quivering its warning. A voice whispered to him in the darkness. Dance with the snake! Dance with the snake! And the snake materialized from the darkness and slithered down his throat and coiled in his belly. Pain wracked his body as shells burst around him, the battle song reaching crescendo. The snake lashed out. And in his dream he spoke the forbidden words – I am afraid, I am afraid, I am afraid...

U. S. Marshal Maxfield Knight awoke from a restless sleep. He dressed, grumbled to himself, and went out to handle the day's business. After a quick breakfast of steak, scrambled eggs, sliced fried potatoes and coffee, he strode onto the boardwalk.

The ladies of the Temperance Union were singing on the hill. There were twelve of them, and they had gained popularity amongst themselves while the residents of Deadwood turned a wary eye to other ventures. This was a gambler's town and a prospector's town and it was a whore's town; but nature took its course and infused in this hamlet the idea that civilization might flourish, or so the ladies were telling people, and now they were singing gospel songs at Wild Bill's grave.

The sharp, metallic *tink!* sounded from the Chinese Tin Shop as Knight strolled passed toward the waiting stagecoach. Deadwood was also a town busy with commerce. The shopkeepers were evident every ten feet. Food, liquor, women, and a game of cards were available for those tired of prospecting. There was something for everyone. But the singing on the hillside cemetery drifted down with a warbling tone that made him want to leave in a hurry. If those ladies kept up that singing Wild Bill was sure to rise up from his grave and gun them down.

An hour earlier he'd sat in the Oyster Bar on Lee Street and drank two bottles of Deadwood's Golden Nugget beer, not because he wanted it, but because coffee was in short supply. He would have to wait for his coffee until they reached the first switching station thirty miles southwest of here. The previous evening he'd sat with Seth Bullock and listened to a sad story about gold robberies.

"I know riding shotgun isn't your preference, but it'll be an easy ride." Seth Bullock had said to him. "And after you get into Wyoming territory you can handle trouble in any manner that you wish."

"People know me." Max had said. "If we draw fire it's because of the gold. Some men don't mind the idea of killing to get what they want."

"Well, are you going to do it or not?"

"I'm obligated as an officer of the law. I'll do it."

"Good."

"Tell me about the passengers."

"Richard Howell and Herbert Reid. Howell works for the Homestake Mining Company. Reid is employed by the Deadwood Bank. Both groups have lost a great deal to robberies. They want something done. You may have some trouble with them."

"How's that?"

"Some men fancy themselves tougher than they are."

"And these two believe bull roping is easy without having tried it."

"Something like that."

"And the gold?"

"One strongbox on the stage, chained on top with the luggage. All rocks. Word is out that box is filled with gold ore and you're here to ensure its safe arrival in Cheyenne."

"Bait for the fish."

That was when the singing began. Knight glanced irritably toward the open doorway. Bullock chuckled.

"You should hear them after a few belts of whiskey. They sound like mewling cats on the prowl."

"I didn't think the Temperance Union allowed the drinking of whiskey."

Bullock chuckled again and sipped his beer.

"In Deadwood a lady's mood changes right quick. They might preach temperance in the morning and provide a mattress service at night."

"I see."

"There's a whore named Darla riding to Cheyenne. She's got enough money because she was a penny pincher. She's young and she might stir up Howell and Reid. You won't have any trouble with Buster, he's the stage driver."

"I'll handle Howell and Reid and I'll tell Darla to keep her skirt down or she'll be walking to Cheyenne."

Bullock's expression turned serious and he leveled his gaze at Knight. "There's one more thing. This half breed, Vincent Two Hatchets; some Indians call him Vincent Two Knives and others yet call him the Tomahawk Killer, and, well, he's a man to watch. He's out there and he'll be wanting that gold. He's contentious as hell. I wouldn't want you to get hurt."

"I've heard what he did. I'll be careful."

"Other than that," Bullock continued, "It'll be an easy ride, like I said. Unless Vincent Two Hatchets gets the better of you, you'll be alright."

"And if he's the one behind the robberies like you suspect?"

"Please kill him."

"I've done plenty of that before." Knight said grimly.

An hour later Knight found himself passing the Chinaman's tin shop. Deadwood was alive with noise. In addition to the warbling of the Temperance Union the air was filled with the din of commerce: The clip-clop of horses and mules; the rattle of a harness; the steady murmur of conversation among the men that often congregated on the boardwalk in groups; and on this afternoon the banal singing of the Ladies Temperance Union.

Knight thought of Wild Bill and the time in Kansas he'd given some of the boys from the seventh cavalry something to think about. Hickok could be a hard man when circumstances warranted, but no man's bones should be subjected to the banshee wailing of menstruating harlots. It was time he rid himself of Deadwood and get on with his mission.

He sent a telegram to Deputy U. S. Marshal Cole Tibbs that said simply: RENDEZVOUS ON TIME. Then he stopped at the livery to check on his horse. Satisfied that the animal was well cared for he retrieved his 73' Winchester from the storage room, paid in advance, and assured the owner he'd pick up the horse when he could. Then he went out to find the stagecoach near the Hotel.

Buster Dobbs was smoking a cigar as he walked up. Buster was tall and heavy. Blue eyes shone out of a face

12

covered in a graying beard.

"So you'll be the one."

"I guess so."

Dobbs smiled. "Well I've ridden in the shotgun seat myself a time or two. This'll be the first time I've had a marshal with me."

"Where are the passengers?"

"Drinking in one of the cribs. They'll be along shortly."

"Let's hope they don't complicate matters."

Knight looked over the stagecoach. It was an old Wells Fargo & Company carriage. The Wells Fargo Stage line had sold its carriages years ago and preferred leaving the difficult work of mail transport to regional carriers. In this instance, it was the Cheyenne Stage & Express Company that operated the stagecoach from Deadwood. Their route would take them into Wyoming to the Canyon Springs Stage Station, across the Platte River and on to Cheyenne. The carriage itself still carried the fading Wells Fargo letters on its door. The brass luggage bars atop the carriage were newly polished. Two cases sat atop the coach. Knight made note of the fact there was room on top for him to sit. He might even use the luggage as a barrier. The interior had been newly upholstered, and at no small expense. The usual hard-wood benches were cushioned like a settee. The passengers would ride in relative comfort. A team of six black horses were tethered to their harnesses and swishing their tails nervously.

A few minutes later two men that had to be Howell and Reid approached the coach as Knight completed his inspection. Both men were middle-aged and overweight. They struck Knight as pompous. The first man introduced himself as Richard Howell. His thick mane of hair was graying at the temples, like flecks of ash.

The second man had less hair and a round, pasty face and double-chin. His head reminded Knight of a loaf of bread that had baked too long and settled at an odd angle. This was Herbert Reid. Both men shook hands with weak grips, an indication to Knight they were spineless and easily manipulated. A man's handshake should be as firm as his word. The two shook hands like dance hall girls but Howell said in a gruff voice: "Let's get moving. We won't dally any longer than we have to." And Reid, perhaps feeling the need to make an impression, added: "Indeed! The sooner we engage the situation the sooner we can resolve this matter. Shall we embark?"

"There's a woman coming along," Knight said. "We'll leave when she gets here."

"That'll be Miss Anderson walking our way now," Buster said.

Darla Anderson was dressed like a schoolmarm, prim and proper with a high collar and a plain brown jacket over her starched blouse. Her skirt was equally plain and Knight never would have mistaken her for a whore. She was pretty enough, and that would work to her advantage if she wanted it to.

Knight introduced himself, and she answered demurely, "Pleased to meet you. I hadn't known a lawman would be riding with us."

"Just a precaution, ma'am. Nothing to worry about."

Howell and Reid were polite and gentlemanly but expressed their eagerness to get moving. Knight stole a glance at Dobbs who appeared ready to laugh. The two men climbed into the coach followed by Darla and Knight took his seat next to Dobbs. He cradled his Winchester in his arms.

"I have my shotgun under the seat." Dobbs said. "It's good to have a shotgun along." He pulled a wad of chewing

14

tobacco from his stained buckskin pocket and gnawed off a piece.

Knight frowned. "I expect since I'm riding in the shotgun seat that's solid advice."

"That '73 is a mighty fine rifle. Damn near as good as my old Henry. We gave those rebel bastards a hard time with those Henry rifles."

"I expect we did." Knight said. He tried not to think about the war. This journey would take them into another type of war, one he had chosen to fight when he accepted the star of a United States Marshal's service.

"I had that Henry rifle with me when General Sherman marched us through Georgia." Dobbs continued. "Those rebels said our Henry rifles could be loaded on Sunday and fired all week." Dobbs chuckled. Knight glanced at Buster when he said the general's name.

"I was there." Knight said flatly.

"Yup, I heard about you. I heard Carleton Usher was a mean sonofabitch."

"He was," Knight said.

Reid had stuck his head out of the coach window and said gruffly, "Hey old timer! Let's get going before Christmas!"

Dobbs looked down over his right shoulder at Reid and said "Hay is for horses!" before spitting a brown stream of tobacco juice in Reid's direction. Dobbs chortled happily. "That set him straight! He pulled his head back like a turtle into his shell."

And with that Dobbs lashed his whip and flicked the reins and the horses set out. They rolled out of Deadwood and the metallic *tink!* from the Chinese tin shop began to fade. Knight had always hated that sound. It reminded him of the confederate lead balls fired from those Virginia flintlock rifles as they smashed into a canteen or a careened off an iron wagon brace. Atlanta burned again briefly in Knight's memory and then he focused on the trail ahead.

They slipped into Wyoming not long after and began the tedious trek south. Days like this Knight thought about that long ago summer when General Sherman marched them south and on to Atlanta in the autumn. Some afternoons the sky was a gentle blue like this and Knight wondered then why his life had become a series of travels across such beautiful country but always culminating in violence. He thought perhaps it was his destiny to travel under a clear sky only to meet death along the trail.

Howell and Reid bothered him. Their presence in the coach nagged at him like an insistent fly. That they were pompous wasn't unusual as Knight felt that most businessmen acted bigger than their britches, but the set-up was wrong. There was no reason for them to take this ride unless they wanted to prove something.

Knight gestured with his thumb down at the coach and asked Buster, "Have these two taken the ride before?"

Buster nodded. "First time together. You think they might be a part of this?"

Knight understood what Buster meant by *this*.

"We'll see." Knight said. "Stage robbing usually makes men dead before it makes them rich."

By agreement they camped that first night twenty miles from Mule Creek. Dinner consisted of hot coffee and cold biscuits which Knight and Buster were accustomed to. Afterward Howell and Reid made a point of mentioning to each other that the madam of the Green Door was skilled in the culinary arts as well as the boudoir. Knight ignored their chatter. They had been given notice that a late start would bring them short of the switching station at Mule Creek. They would sleep in bedrolls and take turn at watch. After ten o'clock the campfire would be allowed to burn low

16

without rekindling.

Darla kept to herself saying little. The men were polite and Knight had a gut feeling that both Howell and Reid knew Darla better than they were letting on. The three of them we relaxed around each other.

Both Howell and Reid wanted to take the first watch which was always the easiest. Since Knight doubted either man could stay awake he placed Reid on first watch followed by Buster. Howell would take third watch and Knight planned on shaking him loose early. Any attack would logically come late. Once a camp was settled it became vulnerable.

With the Black Hills behind them the landscape tapered into a grassy plain punctuated by small, rolling hills. There were a trees and scrub where a tactician might take aim with a rifle. Knight made note of this knowing there wasn't much he could do. The previous robberies had been directed at the stagecoach itself, stopping its journey, and only using violence as a last resort. They would be braced from the side or front at gunpoint but Knight wouldn't take any chances and offer up the bait easily.

They un-harnessed the horses and hobbled them in a swell of grass. Buster prepared the bedrolls. They would sleep spread out around the fire. The coach itself would serve as a barricade should there be gunfire. Of course Knight didn't like it but he had a sense now there was a story unknown to him, and surviving encounters with outlaws was sometimes reliant on understanding their story.

The western summer sky was alive with color. Once the sun slid below the tree-line the horizon gives up a wave of red and orange that leaps across the sky with startling clarity. Knight thought that sometimes it appears the horizon is burning. A red sky in the morning foretold of danger, or so an ancient seaman had once told him. At twilight the blue deepens and this, for Knight, was the loneliest time for he saw then into mankind's past, where nature held dominion over an insignificant platoon, and the coming darkness would test every man's sanity. The falling of light into a dark abyss elicited from him a hollow feeling; a sense of uselessness that had not left him since the war. His thumb reflexively stroked the hammer of his Colt.

Soon enough, he thought.

And with the darkness came the stars that burned coldly and brought another type of loneliness. He slept lightly through Reid's watch, one eye perpetually open and his senses alert for any unusual night sounds. There was the wind and the distant chatter of birds which diminished as the sky darkened. Animal sounds murmured amongst the black silhouettes of spindly trees and flung about with an uneven cadence that rose and fell between the small hills.

As expected, Reid's watch was uneventful and when Buster took his place Knight allowed himself to sleep. The old drover would be sensible and rouse him if he felt even a twinge of uncertainty.

He wanted to dream about his childhood because it had disturbed him for some years that he couldn't remember the sound of his mother's voice. He saw her round face, the clear green eyes, the sandy hair colored by the sun and touched by a streak of gray that a prairie woman earned in her first childbirth, but her voice was lost to him.

At least in his childhood there was the absence of guns and he might see images of the farm or the long green sparkle of the Illinois river on a summer's day. If he thought about these things sometimes he would experience a moment of clarity and the sky framed behind his mother's lean body would give up clouds that drifted past like daffodil puffs along the blue horizon. That was his favorite memory. He must have been ten and his mother was smiling. It was the barn raising and the neighbors had come for miles to help his father raise the barn on that long ago June day.

He could hear the sound of hammers pounding nails, the drone of voices although he couldn't make out any words. He smelled the food. The potatoes in the basket and the bread and the goose they devoured greedily. Later, the men stood in the sun and their shirts were soiled by their sweat, their perspiring red faces sunburned and then the smell of the corn whiskey they slurped from glass jars.

Long before the war.

Long before his memory of the sky was punctuated by black artillery smoke that drifted past like small thunderclouds, his ears ringing from the sound of napoleon shells bursting at the tree line or the whine of a minnie ball before it torc through bone.

Something changed inside him when he thought about the war. He was also prone to recalling with clarity the faces of the men he'd killed: Jake Grimstone, Carleton Usher, Juno Eckstrom, Silas Manchester and others. When he heard Buster talking with Howell a few hours later he immediately propped himself on his elbows, pushed himself upward and he was on his feet. Buster came out of the darkness and stretched himself on the ground where he pulled his blanket over himself. His head turned and he looked at Knight.

"That damn fool lit himself a cigar when he came on watch. Any vaqueros out yonder had to see that."

"He put it out?"

Buster chortled. "That he did."

Knight went out of the camp and quickly found Howell forty feet from the perimeter as Knight had instructed. He made a point of scuffing his boot on a rock as he approached and as Howell turned in his direction Knight

19

said, "Ease up, Howell."

"Marshal, that damn fool old man almost shot me."

"You light a cigar on watch again and I'll shoot you."

"Now listen here, there's no call for that."

"You make one more mistake and I'll leave you on the trail."

"Why that's plain foolish talk. We don't even know if any robbers will come after us."

Knight hit him in the mouth. Howell went back and stretched out flat on his back. Knight picked up the Winchester and then quickly slipped Howell's Colt from his holster. After a few moments Howell grunted and sat up.

"Keep your voice down." Knight said.

Howell cursed softly and pulled himself to his feet.

"You had no right to hit me." He said softly. He sleeved blood from his lip.

"Go bunk down. You've irritated me enough tonight."

"All right, marshal, but you shouldn't have hit me."

"You talk too much."

Howell limbered away, and the darkness swallowed him. Knight set the Winchester and Colt on a boulder and leaned up against the cold stone to watch the night.

A strong box full of rocks and a half breed that might rob them. That's what this was all about. Bait for an outlaw that Knight figured could not be any wiser than any other outlaw. Maybe Howell was the inside man. But to risk your life for a box of quartz and pebbles if you knew it made no sense. Bullock had told him it would be an easy ride but now he was working a longer sentry duty. Nothing about this was going to be easy.

And so he watched the night unfold which for a long while was akin to watching nothing; but then it was a spell watching the slow shifting of stars and finally the slow dissolve into a lighter sky.

In the morning he gave Howell his Colt back and said, "If you have a grudge we can settle it in Cheyenne like men, but meanwhile you follow my orders and keep your mouth shut." Howell nodded with a forlorn look on his face, but said nothing. No one spoke as they ate a breakfast of beef jerky and coffee, and shortly Dobbs had the horses harnessed. They were on their way again.

Knight was uneasy as the stage rattled along. That uneasiness would stay with him all afternoon. In the bristling blue sky miles behind them he thought he could discern a trail of dust washed by the wind.

Chapter 2

Vincent Two Hatchets began his rendezvous with destiny in the Dakotas. With daylight their camp came alive and the men and women were busy with activities that ensured their survival. He would learn later that the white man began his day with activities that had little to do with survival but much to do with personal gratification.

He did not know his father, the white man named Vincent that had lain with his mother. He was a fur trapper and died in the Black Hills one winter after coming down with a cough. This he learned from his mother, Small Bird, who was taken by Standing Bear when he was sixty. Small Bird would become Standing Bear's last wife and she would give birth to his sister, Willow-Among-the-Grass, who died at the age of ten.

Vincent Two Hatchets enjoyed his memories of his family. He had many cousins and half-brothers in the camp but he thought of them only as *Iwatkusua*, the joking relatives who teased him constantly. He remembered the late summer when he caught three large trout but lost them to a diligent raccoon before he could return to camp. The men called him Cannot Fish in jest and so in his eighth year Cannot Fish began his first lessons with knives and tomahawks. His goal was to slay the raccoon that stole his fish while he slept alongside the stream on a lazy summer's day.

It was a white trader that brought the hatchet that would become his favorite. It had a short, blunt oak handle and a seven-inch span across the blade. With this short-handled hatchet, he killed the raccoon that had stolen his fish. He practiced for hours until he could throw the hatchet with accuracy.

One day he rode with his friend, Red Moccasin, to a settler's camp with instructions to trade a pony for blankets, knives and flour. It was a hot and bright noon under a calico sky, with a warm breeze blowing in from the west, when the two boys rode their ponies into a settlement fifty miles from the Fort Berthold Trading Post. The settlement didn't have a name. It was contrary to the Berthold Post where the United States cavalry often sent troops. The trading post they visited was no more than a mud hut surrounded by a dozen hastily constructed buildings. A few settlers slept in surplus tents pilfered from the army. Cannot Fish and Red Moccasin were wary of encountering soldiers. Their instructions were to avoid the white men at the Berthold Post and trade here from a man name Maltachi.

They led the extra pony by a rope and when they neared the camp the scent of decay assailed them. The settlement stank and they wanted to finish their business quickly and begin their return journey immediately. Two nights under the stars was preferable than staying in a filthy camp such as this.

Maltachi eyed them suspiciously when they entered the hut. He was fat, dark-haired, and sweating as he drank whiskey from a brown jug. He wore no shirt and tufts of black hair clung to his chest like black spider webs. His beard glistened with drool. When they explained they had a pony to trade he grunted, pushed himself off the barrel that had been his perch, and veered from the hut to examine the goods. He liked the pony. A group of men had circled round to watch. Even when Maltachi gestured to a group of surly men with a yellow grin the two boys were oblivious to the danger. Maltachi had traded with the tribe before although this was the first time the two boys had come alone.

A thin, black-toothed man came up and shot Red Moccasin in the head. A shower of blood, brain and skull slapped hotly against Cannot Fish. He was pulled from his pony, his deerskin shirt pulled from his body, and they pistol-whipped him. The man that had just killed Red Moccasin slammed the Colt Navy revolver against his head causing a gash that ran down from his forehead to his right eye. Blood spooled in his eye blurring his vision. He heard a man say "Get 'em!" and another man say "Let's have us some fun!"

They pushed him back and forth, spinning him about until he was dizzy. Crashing to the ground he bit his tongue and blood burst from his mouth.

"The boy's done hurt hisself!"

"Just kill the dog and be done with it."

He heard a revolver's hammer click and the cylinder spin into place but the hammer clacked against a bad percussion cap. A man cursed.

"Don't waste a lead ball on this cur. Lock him up and we'll let the boys have him later."

Their obscene laughter rang in his ears as they dragged him through the weeds and tossed him into a windowless hut. He drifted in and out of consciousness until at last he remembered looking at the sun peeking through the slats and when he next blinked the sun had vanished and night had cloaked the settlement. He rummaged about and found a rusted axe with a short handle. There were sounds of drunken revelry outside and through the slats he could see a bonfire raging. They had taken Red Moccasin's body and hung him upside down from a scaffold. His long hair had caught fire and soon his body was engulfed in flames. The bonfire crackled and the flames spread up the body and burned the scaffold as well.

He studied the men. They were white men and Mexicans and those of an undetermined race. But it made little difference their ancestry. They represented civilization as the white man presented it. The hanging image of Red Moccasin's body would stay with him for a very long time, even after he attempted to live like a civilized man, and so the flames of that unholy night were seared into his very soul.

He used the axe and punched out a few slats, slipping through and away into the darkness. He knew they would look for him. They would seek him on the trail home, and without a rifle he would have little chance of survival. He made his way across a prairie in the direction of the Fort Berthold Trading Post. He hoped they would not think his escape would be made in the direction of a white man's fort. He stayed clear of obvious trails, guiding himself by the stars. He was safe enough under cover of darkness but come morning they would begin hunting him. He found a rocky terrain and exploited its usefulness in preventing footprints. He changed his gait and stride when crossing a field of grass to better emulate the passage of deer.

When the sky turned pale he sought a place to hide. The first day would foretell his fate and so he considered every option. He decided to bury himself in a rocky hillside. He found a crevice in plain view not half a mile from the trail to Fort Berthold. He went to a stream and dug at the muddy embankment. He covered himself in mud. He made tracks near the stream to confuse them, and then he gathered an armful of fallen branches and took them to the crevice. He wedged himself inside the crevice and stationed the branches in a haphazard fashion as cover. The crevice was tight and he was uncomfortable. But any curious traveler might peer into the crevice and see only dirt and wind-blown branches. The sun would be behind him most of the day. He was essentially in plain view, but invisible.

His body ached from the beating he had taken but he resolved to survive. The rusted axe he carried with him but left now on the ground in the crevice. He was too tired to hold it any longer. The morning passed uneventfully and he slept fitfully, his body prevented him from falling by the crags that pressed against his sore ribs.

In the afternoon he heard horses out past the sound of birdsongs and the breeze-ruffled grass. They were not close but he waited anxiously. Eventually he saw a group of riders in the distance. They reined to a halt and a solitary rider broke off from the group. He cantered his horse to within thirty yards of Cannot Fish. It was the thin, black-toothed man that had killed Red Moccasin. The man slid from his horse and studied the ground and surrounding area, his eyes touching on Cannot Fish but his gaze swept past, the illusion having worked. The man stood there calmly in the sunlight and urinated. Cannot Fish resisted the urge to leap from his hiding place and kill the man with his axe.

The man remounted his horse and joined his friends. They rode east and Cannot Fish waited an hour before moving. The sun was hot on his back but he felt invigorated. He found a hill that gave him a good perspective on the area but riders were gone. A plan formulated in his mind then, and he prepared himself for what he knew must happen. Later that afternoon he killed a rabbit, skinned it as best he could with the axe and ate the meat raw. He would not light a fire. Now he planned on staying alive in order to exact his vengeance.

He remained where he was, content that from here he would be safe until he chose to move again. He waited two days. He lived on rabbits and small birds that he killed with stones or by hurtling the axe with practiced ease. He waited until twilight on the third day before making his way back to the trading post. The night was cold but now the mud that remained caked to his chest helped warm him. There was another bonfire burning and drunken revelers talking loudly. He waited amongst the scrub and small trees, always invisible in the night, a shadow that moved stealthily, the axe clutched in his hand.

It was late when he slipped through the shadows and went around to the rear of an adobe hut. Through the small window he could see the man that had killed Red Moccasin standing behind another man who had his pants around his ankles. The man was leaning over a table while Red Moccasin's killer heaved himself at the man's buttocks, grunting. The sight of them and their moans made Cannot Fish sick to his stomach. When they finished, both men pulled up their trousers and set to drinking from a brown jug. They were sitting at a table that faced the front door. Cannot Fish slipped in the rear door, coming up behind Red Moccasin's killer and cleaved his skull in half with a mighty sweep of the axe. The second man, who was a much drunker man, struggled to rise from his seat. Cannot Fish had to pull the axe free because it had lodged tightly in the dead man's skull. There was just enough time to beat the other man to death with two hard swipes. The man had a small hatchet in his belt, and so he removed it and used that to chop off the men's hands. They would not have hands in the after-life, and so their deaths rendered them useless.

He didn't know their names and he didn't care. The man he wanted to kill next was Maltachi. The big sleazy man had disappeared.

A few days later he had rejoined his people and told them about Red Moccasin's death, and how he had avenged him with the axe. He had the bloody axe to show them, and, in fact, word had gotten around that a crazy Indian had murdered some white men. He also had the small hatchet he had taken. This was the day that Vincent Two Hatchets was born, and even some of his own people feared him from that day on. Some called him Vincent Two Knives and he was known by both names. Vincent Two Hatchets was on a long trail that would bring him face to face with Maxfield Knight, but not before he would come to understand the true meaning of both betrayal and grief.

Vincent wasn't satisfied killing Red Moccasin's murderer. He wanted to kill the man that had given the order, Maltachi. His immediate concern, however, was the systematic elimination of the tribe's way of life by the white men who organized a boarding school. There was much debate among the tribal elders regarding this boarding school, but in the end they had little choice.

Vincent set his mind to studying the white man's ways. They wanted to cut his hair and dress him in a white man's clothes. They wanted to teach him the white man's language. He would learn the language; he would think of this as a weapon. To understand an enemy was a way of gathering strength.

He also listened carefully. He knew enough of the Mexican tongue to get an idea where Maltachi was holed up. Now he could piece together information as the white man's language became familiar to him.

Eventually he learned that Maltachi and his men had

moved their business operation to a village about thirty miles north. They were transporting liquor, guns and horses between trading posts, mostly with stolen material.

The next morning Vincent left without speaking to anyone. Following a thin stream he listened to the rifling sound of the rushing water as night fell. He followed no roads, no trails. He allowed his horse to feel out her own path. He guided her north without hurrying. He knew the place where Maltachi was staying.

The land was dark with only a sliver of moonlight illuminating the landscape. There was just enough light for the Great Spirit to guide him. He saw a deer and then an owl took flight from a tree, its great wings fanning like a row of knives. That was a good omen, Vincent thought.

The settlement was dark when he approached, a single oil lamp visible between the slats of a dilapidated cabin. He could hear voices inside and one of the voices belonged to Maltachi. He left his horse grazing on some brush and approached the cabin silently. There was an outhouse behind the cabin, a small corral on the eastern side. A line of trees and brush bordered the northside. Smoke was drifting from the stone chimney.

Vincent crept to the window and craned his neck for a look inside. Maltachi was at a table drinking and eating the remnants of a pheasant. Another man, thin and smaller, sat with him. A third man was snoring on a cot. Maltachi and the thin man gorged themselves on the bird. They drank from a shared bottle. Maltachi and the thin man looked as if they hadn't bathed in weeks. The room was hazy from smoke.

Maltachi burped and rubbed his extended belly. He stood up, teetering drunkenly. "Gotta go," he muttered. The thin man continued eating without looking up. Vincent recognized his opportunity and quickly went around to the outhouse and slipped inside. He waited until he heard Maltachi stumbling toward the door. When Maltachi yanked the outhouse door open he was greeted by Vincent's tomahawk cleaving his skull in half.

Leaving the body where it fell, his pulled loose his bloody weapon and walked to the cabin where he strode confidently inside. The thin man was gnawing at a piece of pheasant meat and watched Vincent with wide eyes. His mouth was open, bits of meat clinging to his lips. Vincent killed him in his chair while he was holding his dinner in his grimy hands. Two swift hacks and the man's face was torn away, blood and brains splattered across the wood table.

Vincent turned his attention to the third man sleeping on the cot. He decided to allow the man to live. Let him live in fear and let that fear spread when he told people about a ghost killer who came in the night and shattered skulls. The man would wake up and see the bodies and word of the murders would spread.

He felt good at having properly avenged Red Moccasin's murder. He went out to retrieve his horse and the whispering of the trees as the branches swayed in the breeze was like a chant of victory, a cadence that matched the fury of his beating heart.

Two years would pass before he killed another man, and when he did it would change his life forever.

Chapter 3

Deputy U. S. Marshal Cole Tibbs was camped on a hillside in a strand of aspens and birch. He'd spent a month in Raven Flats with his fiancé, Jamie Hart, and at the appointed time he'd ridden to Adobe Springs to wait for Knight's telegram. The aging marshal had been a good friend for several years, and Tibbs enjoyed working with him. The problem was, riding with Max Knight had almost gotten them both killed a few times.

Tibbs and Jamie had been talking about getting married in another year. They'd talked about marriage before, and Jamie wanted him to give up being a lawman and take up shop-keeping. That wasn't going to happen. Ranching, maybe...the fact was, he enjoyed being a lawman.

Setting these thoughts aside, he concentrated on the broad expanse of plains, hills, and arroyos that intersected with each other for hundreds of miles. Wyoming was hard country, with a landscape that changed constantly. A man could spend a day riding across a grassy plain and suddenly find himself spurring his horse through a steep gorge, the Sioux fast on his back trail.

Heat mirages danced out in the tall grass; the line of distant mountains seemed like a medieval fortress. Tibbs didn't like this country no matter that it was beautiful. He didn't like the fact that he was constantly looking over his shoulder anticipating an Indian tomahawk being flung at him. His instincts told him he was being observed, and his skin crawled with a prickly sensation.

Before him the flat plains drifted into the green hills and tangled up with a thickly forested valley. There was no sign of life. No eagles floated in the blue sky; no deer and no bear traipsed along the old trails. They were here, of course, but he couldn't see them. The lack of any sign of life bothered him and added to his anxiety. He had no doubt that Max Knight was involving them both in something that would test both their courage and their skill with a gun.

The way he understood it, Seth Bullock had his hands full in Deadwood, and the recent stagecoach robberies had focused on shipments from the Homestake Mining

Company. Knight went to Deadwood to sort out the details, and Tibbs was assigned the task of following along, and to make certain he wasn't seen following along. Tibbs was the ace card up Knight's sleeve. If the stage was robbed - and they expected a robbery - then Tibbs was to intervene on Knight's behalf.

Good plan, thought Tibbs. But now that he was out here in the big lonesome country, it was obvious that staying out of sight wasn't going to be easy. Not one damn bit. He was sweating and the back of his neck was tingling.

What looked like a level plain from his hillside vantage point was actually a series of hills, and once he was down there his long-distance view would be limited. He wanted to get down about three miles so he could watch the stagecoach pass in two days.

Tibbs didn't like the set-up. It felt wrong.

Edging off the hillside, he turned and followed a trail between the birch trees until he found his camp. His horse was hobbled nearby, chomping at the tall grass.

He stood for a minute by the embers of the fire. The coffee was still warm so he poured himself a cup. He didn't sit down. Instead, he remained standing and slowly circled the camp, sipping at his coffee. All the while he was listening. Birdsongs and the breeze were nudging the maple and birch branches.

All about him nature blossomed and there was no sign of mankind save for his own camp. Cole Tibbs knew this wasn't true. He had been followed, and the acceptance of that fact rang with the clarity of a Sunday church bell.

The land offered a thousand crevices, holes, arroyos, and back-trails where a man could hide. He wasn't going to bother looking for them, but he would have to be aware when they came close. They might have ambushed and killed him already if that had been their intention. They might be following him from simple curiosity, or they might be related to the activities of Vincent Two Hatchets.

He pulled up his camp, put away his supplies, and saddled his horse. He kicked dirt over the still smoking embers of his fire, but made no effort to hide it. They knew where he was. Slow at first, spurring the horse into a trot down the winding trail toward the grasslands. No hurry at all, he thought. Keep going and push along, see what happens.

The landscape was deceptive once he had come down from the hillside. The swells and ridges looked flat from a distance, but once he was riding through them his visibility was limited. A grassy path led him into a swarm of birch and then along a rocky switchback. The temperature changed from cold to warm as the sun began to beat down at him.

The air changed, too; ceasing the gentle nudge he felt on the hillside, the air was now tight and dry. Sound echoed dully across the landscape. The birds seemed further away. His horse whinnied once nervously.

A quarter mile at a trot; a mile. When a cloud drifted across the sun the land became ominous. His horse's ears twitched.

Hills on each side of him; and the trail he followed was no more than some worn animal path. No buffalo, no deer in sight. Grass and dirt and sky greeted him at every step. Spindly trees and scrub brush loomed at him and not even the sunlight could make the scene look pleasant. Not when you know you're being tracked.

The thing of it is, Tibbs thought, is that I don't know what they want. They can kill me at any time with a rifle. I wouldn't hear the shot. They could drop me right now.

He yanked on the reins and brought the horse to a halt. Far off, another horse whinnied. The sound damn near blended into the sunlight to be swept away by the stifling heat. He could smell the pungent grass and scrub-brush. In that hot bowl of air and heat and the scent of the land there had been a horse whinnying.

A flutter of wings sounded with sudden fury. His horse snorted, raised up startled as a pheasant flung itself from the weeds and flapped loudly away.

Tibbs waited, regulating his breathing, keeping calm. His trackers were far enough away. At least that's what he was gambling on. Then the wind picked up and a feather came floating across his line of sight. He watched it, perplexed. The feather wasn't from the pheasant. It was black and it spun in a vortex, coming close to him. It landed in the grass about twenty feet in front of him.

He spurred the horse and approached it. He looked down at the black feather and a chill swept down his spine. His eyes swept across the sky and saw nothing. The silent world around him was suddenly foreboding.

He rode on, but slowly. He let his horse pause and nibble at the grass. He felt like a trespasser although he wasn't certain why. Perhaps it was his feeling that he wasn't welcome here. The silence and impending sense of danger hung over him like a cloak.

He wanted to confront his unseen pursuers, and he was angry at their lack of activity. He felt exactly like a mouse being batted around by a cat. Tibbs didn't like that feeling at all.

A half mile was achieved with agonizing slowness. Then he saw two figures on horseback on a swell of tall grass off on his left. He blinked and the two figures were gone.

They were much closer to him than he'd expected. Two Sioux warriors, maybe in their late twenties. Both were clad in buckskin and carried Henry rifles.

He continued cantering forward. There was no sense in stopping. They had already made up their minds on what they'd do, and now Tibbs was faced with waiting them out. His own Winchester rifle was in a scabbard; the leather tong was off his Colt's hammer. He kept his hands on the reins and tried not to look obvious when his peripheral vision snapped left and right.

Thirty minutes passed. An hour. He was making no progress. At some point he would have to make a camp and wait for the stagecoach.

An hour later he chose a location up in a thick clump of birch. It was the best defensive position he could manage. The hill gave him the high ground and the trees provided cover.

Two against one isn't so bad, he thought to himself.

Two against one. Hell, he'd faced worse odds when he joined Knight against Silas Manchester and fifty men in the Rocky Mountains.

Cole Tibbs was no coward, but he understood fear. That was what he felt as he hobbled his horse and prepared his camp.

Tibbs and Knight had gone up against Carleton Usher and his sons in Raven Flats, and they had survived. Knight had survived being held captive in a mining labor camp run by Juno Eckstrom, and he had faced Jake Grimstone, killing him in wild, vicious battle that added to Knight's reputation as a fearless lawman. That, at least was true. Tibbs looked at Knight as one of the toughest men he'd ever met. His guts and determination often gave Tibbs reason to pause, and Tibbs wasn't usually one to be in awe of other men. Knight was different.

He also knew that Maxfield Knight was a man plagued by ghosts. The death of his wife had changed him, and he'd heard the story how Knight had tracked down her killers one by one. Even before then, at Shiloh, Knight had felt the flames.

Knight himself was reticent, but the stories got out. Tibbs suspected that most everything he'd heard about the man was true. What little Knight did talk about simply confirmed his reputation. What Tibbs had seen was proof enough.

It was late in the afternoon and his camp was made, and Tibbs was ready to fight. The light was good, and his view of the surrounding area was clear. In fact, the afternoon was tranquil, a warm breeze had come up and nudged the trees. The sound of leaves whispering in the sunlight offered a drowsy feeling of contentment.

There was no sign of those two Indians. Tibbs waited, alert to any sudden movement or sound. Nothing happencd.

When the sun was lower he watched the shadows lengthen, and that's when he expected them to attack. The light faded into a lavender twilight, and still nothing happened.

He abstained from making a fire. When the light was gone and night had taken a firm hold of the landscape, he waited in the darkness with his rifle ready.

There were rustling sounds in the brush; an owl hooted. The stars were clear in the firmament, and still nothing happened.

All night he waited, and he dozed a bit, always expecting an attack, but that attack never came. In the morning he surveyed the area and there was no sign of the two braves. He ate cold biscuits and drank water from his canteen.

He saddled his horse and set out to rendezvous with Max Knight.

He rode all morning, and he was tired from not

sleeping. It wasn't until after three o'clock that afternoon when he saw the two Indians again. They were on horseback about a half mile out, far on his right. They were riding parallel of him, taking their time.

Tibbs wondered to himself: *What has the marshal gotten me into?*

Chapter 4

When Vincent Two Hatchets was fifteen years old he fell in love with a half breed girl name Aiyana. Little was known of her white father but her mother had been Aponi, a Lakota woman who was ugly and never thought clearly. She spread her legs for any man that would feed her and that was how she survived until the age of twenty-five when she gave birth to Aiyana. Aponi died giving her daughter life, and Aiyana was named by the Christian missionaries who confused tribal names and tribal history.

Vincent knew her from the white man's school which he hated. They lived in the Christian buildings that separated them, but they walked to school together. Their lives were orderly but the Christians were not friendly people.

Vincent never talked with Aiyana about his hatred for the white men. He was taken by her simple beauty and with her at his side his mind was focused on her. She was gentle but highly intelligent. She had learned to read the white man's language faster than he had. She understood arithmetic. Her eyes carried a light of innocence and wonder at the world around her, and this joy she expressed in simple declarations. She might marvel over a clump of weeds that she said were flowers, and even the Christian teachers said she had a gift for understanding nature.

She understood the land and this impressed Vincent.

She cooked as well as any of the older women; she could stitch a torn leather shirt and skin a rabbit without complaint. The sight of blood didn't bother her.

It took time for him to realize that the white men despised mixed bloods with greater disdain than any other people. They hated all Indians, but the Christians had a special and perverse hatred they reserved for Indians of mixed blood. He could not fathom a reason for this hatred, but it was there every single day. He witnessed a boy being flogged by the priest for simply refusing to answer a question. Vincent knew the boy struggled with English and wasn't the type to speak quickly, all facts that were irrelevant to white men. His bare-back was whipped by the priest with a fervor that reminded Vincent of the violent lust he'd seen in too many men. The priest enjoyed himself. With every lash his sweating face gleamed with pleasure, his eyes glazed with an inner vison that made the priest look like a madman. This was what their Christ wanted, this was the path to Jesus, this was what their God desired most of all, and Vincent was horrified.

Knowledge of the white man's world such as this was at odds with his idyllic love for Airyana. The nuns and the priest talked about the love of Jesus but instead gave them hatred and torture.

"You half breeds need to work harder than the others," the priest told him once. "You have to make up for that poison that's in your blood."

The priest's name was Edwin Felton and Vincent came to view him as an evil wraith loping about in his long black cloak dispensing tortures on any Lakota who displeased him. Aiyana told him there was a twelve-year old girl named Meyne who unwillingly shared Felton's bed.

Yet that first summer of their marriage was a gentle memory, the only such memory in Vincent's life. He was put to work tending the gardens and helping around the farm that served to supply the Christians with food. Vincent spoke calmly and respectfully to Felton and the nuns, and in response they left him and Aiyana alone. Vincent ignored their so-called generous Lord and tended to his own garden of love which was imminently pleasing compared to the hateful rhetoric of Father Felton.

In late summer when the sun had changed and the afternoon light seemed distant and autumn was approaching, Aiyana came to him and said that she would give him a child. This was the same week that Meyne hung herself in the kitchen of the school building where Farther Felton also had his office and where the youngest children slept on bunks in a big room. Aiyana still attended Bible classes and she sometimes talked about the goodness of Jesus having come to accept some of the white man's teachings. Aiyana told Vincent what the nuns had said about Meyne hanging herself and that it was from having Satan in her belly.

Aiyana said that Meyne would not hang herself and they knew from looking at her unclothed body when they washed her corpse before the burial that a child was in her belly. They all believed that the priest had killed her but they said nothing. Aiyana explained to Vincent that it was a way of knowing things that the Christians said was believing in their Lord, a way of faith of knowing without proof. They said nothing and Meyne was buried in the graveyard behind the school and Father Felton read meaningless words from the Bible. The graves had no markers.

Autumn brought the corn harvest which was difficult because of a drought. The land was too dry and the corn was thin. It would be a difficult winter but they would manage with the flour, beef and supplies the Christians brought from the southeast. All that winter they had just enough and Vincent made certain that Aiyana had more than her share.

Aiyana continued teaching English to the younger students and Vincent, who had become lean but muscular, worked at whatever task was asked of him. He despised the Christians but had reached a point where he managed to live with them for the benefit of Aiyana. The snow was high that year but there was wood for the fire and coal for the pot-bellied stove, and they stayed warm with each other.

Aiyana began bleeding in early April. The baby wasn't due for several weeks but she was feeling some pain, and there was blood. Vincent left the cabin early the following morning and trudged through the melting snow to fetch Doctor Samuel Cornwell from the town of Shannon's Corner. He reached Cottonwood Creek across from the town three hours later. Shannon was a two-street town on a wagon trail that led north to Rapid City.

Vincent asked the old man at the livery where Doc Cornwell's office was and the old man eyed him with bloodstained pupils lacking in kindness. His unshaven face and yellow pallor made Vincent think the old coot was soon to die of consumption which would rid the world of another unfriendly white man.

"Don't you belong in the Pine Hill Christian School? We ain't got too many Indian boys come this way, and when they do they don't last long."

Vincent's belted tomahawks were covered by his buckskin coat and he wanted to shatter the man's skull but he had to think of Aiyana.

"I learned how to read the Bible. I need to see the doctor about my wife."

Experience had taught Vincent to keep white men at arm's length by mentioning the Bible. It was what they wanted to hear.

"That's good to know you heathens are getting some religion. Go down the street past the Silver Dollar Hotel, and right across from that is the Dentist and Tonsorial Parlor. The Doc is in the next building. You'll read his name on a shingle."

Vincent thanked the man and went out to find the doctor. He was an object of curiosity for the townspeople as he passed, but they left him alone. He found the shingle with Dr. Cornwell's name and walked in without knocking. He was in a pleasant drawing room and the doctor was in another room across from him with the door open as he wrote on a parchment with a quill pen. The doctor looked up in surprise, pushed himself to his feet and strode up to Vincent looking aggravated.

"What do you want?" He asked sharply, "I don't tend to Indians."

A white man's eyes. They stared at him with contempt. They peered at him with the haughty gaze of a man that deemed himself superior to all others.

Vincent felt his pulse quicken and he was sweating beneath his buckskin shirt.

"My wife," Vincent began, "she will have a baby. There was some blood. She has some pain..."

"Are you deaf, you damn fool? I don't tend to Indians. Where are you from?"

"Pine Hill."

"Well, I stopped seeing your kind at Pine Hill because it doesn't pay. Father Felton knows that. He never should have sent you. Another doctor is being hired from up near Deadwood. He's a whiskey sodden bastard but he might help. Go find him."

"Sir, please...I'm sorry, but there's no time. I have money, if you can..."

Doc Cornwell turned abruptly on his heel and strode to his desk, pulled open a drawer and retrieved a derringer. Holding the gun straight out and stiff-armed, the doctor walked toward Vincent with the two muzzles pointing at his head.

"I don't tend to Indians and I certainly don't have time for an Indian whore!"

Vincent held up his hands pleadingly. "No, no. She has some white blood; she will have our baby..."

"God almighty you thundering fool! I should shoot you right now just to rid the world of you! I don't care about some half breed Indian whore! Now get out! Do you hear me? I said get out!"

Vincent knew at that moment that he would kill the doctor. Not that day, but one day after their baby was born and after all of this was behind him, he would come when Aiyana was teaching the children the white man's tongue and kill the fool who stood before him now.

Vincent backed away, his own gaze never leaving the doctor's face. He wanted to remember the undisguised contempt on the doctor's features because one day he would turn that contempt to fear.

He willed his anger aside and Aiyana was first and foremost in his mind on the long walk home. He studied the sky and saw rain clouds which would be good for the garden. The white men said the dark clouds were an omen but in their fear of the Great Spirit they failed to see the benefit of rain.

He would pass the road to Pine Hill School and decided to see Father Felton and ask for assistance. The priest could send for the other doctor. When he approached the school the nuns stepped aside and made a path for him. Something in his face told them to keep quiet. He thought they should see him as an omen on a gray day where the clouds made Christians quake with fear.

Father Felton made no overtures but at least he was polite.

"Doc Win Harley can be here in two days if he's sober. I can send a telegram in the morning. It'll cost you ten dollars."

"Ten dollars?"

"Treating your kind costs money. We educate you, feed you and help you find the good Lord, and what thanks do we get? You heathens breed like rats. Ten dollars to help a childbirth case. The school will take five. Doc Harley will spend his five on bottles, but that's his business."

"You'll send the telegram in the morning?"

"You heard me say I would. Are you deaf?"

That was the second time that day that a white man had asked Vincent if he was deaf. He went home and his heart was heavy because now he knew the harsh truth of the white man's world. He had known this already, of course, but now that he saw it again he wouldn't forget.

The cabin was cold when he walked in. The fire had dwindled to embers and Vincent added fresh wood and restarted it, blowing at the embers to bring the fire alive, thinking that Aiyana had fallen asleep. She was on the bunk in the corner and he saw that she was only lightly breathing.

He approached her and touched her arm. She didn't move. He spoke to her but she never flinched. He touched her face and she was too cold. He lifted an eyelid and knew that she was dying. Her eyes were unfocused and their brightness was fading. When he pulled the blanket away from her body he saw the blood. She had lost the baby.

Grief changes a man. For Vincent the grief was a flash of anger that grew into a raging storm. Aiyana looked small and fragile in death, the opposite of her vibrant and enthusiastic personality. Her left eye was partially open, an orb of cold glass, and he brushed his fingers over her eyelids. His hands were shaking as he wrapped her body in several blankets. Aiyana, his love, his life, was stiff and cold and so the tears fell from his eyes, his jaw clenched shut.

An inferno raged in his soul. She had taken their child with her and he wondered if the false Gods of the Christians were pleased with these circumstances. Leaving her body on the bed for a moment, he rummaged about the cabin and took what he knew he needed – knives, a rifle, a box of cartridges, more blankets, the sack of flour and beans.

He placed these items in a sack and left his bride wrapped in blankets on the bed while he walked toward the Pine Hill School. It was twilight when he saw the oil lamps burning in the second floor windows. It was dinner time so he wasn't surprised when he entered the building and ascended the stairs without encountering anyone. He knew they were in the dining hall, and he knew that Father Felton took his meals in the privacy of his office.

When Vincent entered the room the priest must have seen something in his intruder's eyes that sent a shock through him because he immediately opened a desk drawer and brought up a gun. Vincent moved swiftly and struck Felton's hand with his tomahawk, severing two fingers. The priest howled in pain as the gun fell from his bloodied hand. To shut him up, Vincent used the flat side of his tomahawk and bashed Felton across the side of the head which sent him flying backwards where he dropped like a sack.

The sight of Felton's severed fingers was inspiration enough for Vincent to chop off the remaining fingers on both of Felton's hands. He picked up the ten bloody fingers and wrapped them in his bandanna. Felton, who was semi-conscious, stared at him in horror. He mouth opened and closed as he tried to scream, but all that came out of his throat was a gurling whine.

"Tell them all what I did here. Tell them I will come for them all, one by one. Tell that Vincent is at war with all white men."

Vincent spoke in nearly a whisper, and Felton's chest heaved with each breath he took, tears streaming down his face. Vincent didn't look back as he went out and down the stairs. Once outside, he went to the barn and saddled a horse, and then a took a pack mule and tied a rope to its bridle. He heard the nuns screaming inside by the time he was riding away.

He rode home and entered the cabin. He looked at Aiyana's bundled body but said nothing. When he was ready, he lifted her in his arms and carried her outside where he draped her body over the mule. He used an old hemp rope to tie her body in place. Aiyana had been dead for the span of three hours when Vincent Two Hatchets set their cabin on fire.

He knew they would be looking for him. He had let the priest live to tell them, but they wouldn't come until the morning. He mounted his horse and took the mule's rope and rode to Shannon's Corner in the dark. Vincent was exhausted but he had one purpose now, and that was taking his vengeance.

When he arrived at Shannon's Corner is reined his horse and mule to a halt outside the livery, and the old man, who must have heard the them, came out to see about the noise. Vincent slid out of the saddle and split the old man's skull in two so quickly that he didn't think the man knew what hit him.

Killing white men, he thought, was much too easy. He decided on a course of action for Doc Cornwell and a few minutes later he tied his horse and his mule to the hitching rail outside Cornwell's office. He went swiftly inside.

Once again using the flat side of his tomahawk, he knocked Cornwell senseless. By the time Cornwell had regained conscious, Vincent had tied his hands behind his back. He gagged the doctor with his own bandanna and dragged him outside.

"This is my wife," Vincent said, pointing at the bundle of blankets that covered Aiyana, "and you'll ride here with her. You should be honored. If you try to run away I'll kill you."

He helped the bound and frightened doctor onto the mule and then tied him to the bridle. Doc Cornwell was bleeding profusely by being struck in the head. Vincent thought he must have struck him too hard. The man was babbling scnsclcssly through his gag.

"You can service yourself with your own medicine when we get to my camp."

Doc Cornwell blubbered a muffled response through his gag, his eyes wide with fear.

The camp that Vincent had decided on was deep in the forest near Horse Creek. He would be out of sight for the night. He thought about Aiyana and he knew that her spirit was in a better place, and one day he would join her. But not now. Not when a rage burned hotly in his belly.

There was no moon that night but Vincent skillfully guided the horse and mule into the forested hills. The dark trees cradled them and hid them from view. His trail would be easy to follow in the morning. He would be long gone by then, but they would find the doctor.

He made camp in a small clearing and he pulled the doctor off the mule. He carried Aiyana's body and set it next to where he would sleep. Then he lashed a rope around the doctor's ankles, looped the rope around a tree limb and hoisted him upward so that he swing upside down. His head was only half a foot from the ground but there was nothing he could do with his hands tied. The doctor blinked his eyes rapidly as he watched Vincent make a fire.

"I hope you are warm," Vincent said. There was neither sarcasm nor concern in his voice.

Vincent sat for a while next to Aiyana and the doctor could hear him singing or chanting something in his native tongue. When Vincent was ready he took a tomahawk in his hand and stood before the doctor.

"When I cut open your belly your intestines will fall out and that's what you will see as you bleed out. This is your medicine, a coward that sees his own death."

Vincent made three crosshatch swipes with his gleaming tomahawk and the doctor screamed as his belly opened and his bloody guts dangled before his face.

Vincent Two Hatchets, the Tomahawk Killer, the man some called Two Knives, disappeared that night into the Badlands with his beloved wife's body wrapped in blankets and draped over a mule. It didn't take long for his legend to spread. Some Comanche spoke of seeing him a year later; they watched him but never approached him. They said that his wife's ghost walked with him in the Badlands and at night she sang to the cold stars. Gold prospectors encountered him and they feared him and fled the area. Other prospectors had been found butchered and only fools followed the trail of the Tomahawk Killer. No lawmen went looking for him and his Wanted dodger went unclaimed. There was a thousand-dollar bounty on Vincent's head but no bounty hunter pursued him. The rumor circulated that he had died. How could a man survive in the Badlands? Vincent Two Hatchets had become a myth.

He wasn't seen again until six years later when he

robbed the Deadwood Stagecoach carrying the payroll of the Homestake Mining Company. Around his neck he wore a necklace of human finger bones.

Chapter 5

The stage wheeled on toward Cheyenne and marshal Knight was poised and alert in the shotgun seat. His own legend had started to spread across the Western camps and one dime novelist had written a fanciful story about him titled *Showdown at Snakebite Creek* and Seth Bullock had shown it to him six months earlier.

"You're makin' a name for yourself. You and my friend Theodore Roosevelt. Try and avoid ending up like Wild Bill."

"I'll do what I can."

The fact was, staying alive was becoming a chore. Yet he was driven by a passion to see justice done that it was impossible to turn in his badge. The goddamn challenge spurred him onward. He was a man possessed, and he knew it. Maybe this was how he wanted it, a mistake apprehending some outlaw, a quick bullet and a dusty grave.

He shook his head and scowled at the ridgeline miles ahead and wondered if that was the place where they'd be ambushed.

"What the hell has got you all pissed off like a mountain lion?" Buster Dobbs said as he turned his head to his right and spit a long brown stream of tobacco juice into the wind which trailed back and flopped like a worm into the dust. Dobbs chuckled.

"I was thinking that ridgeline ahead of us doesn't look good."

"Hell, marshal, none of this wild country looks good

47

when you know you've got Indians and robbers plannin' on shooting holes in you, or worse!" Dobbs let out another mirthful snort. "That ridgeline is called Cemetery Hill by stage line drivers because so many Pony Express riders got ambushed up there back in the day. We'll see a few markers but it's mostly dust. No stage drivers have died there yet and I don't plan on being the first. You keep that shotgun handy and stay awake."

"I won't doze off."

"No, I expect you won't. You look mean as hell and ready to shoot any rattlesnake that crosses the road."

"That's about right."

"Fire me up a smoke from the makin's in my pocket here and help yourself."

Knight took the small pouch and rolled two cigarillos for them, taking his time because the bumpy road made it difficult. He managed to get it done without losing tobacco. He struck a wooden match on his trouser leg and puffed both tobacco sticks to life. Dobbs took his and puffed merrily away.

"You aughta tell me about killing Juno Eckstrom. I heard that sonofabitch was meaner than a hungry iguana!"

A year earlier Knight had learned that three gunfighters, J. T. Parker, Laramie Calhoun and Lee Taylor, had reappeared and Knight knew that meant trouble. Knight and Parker's friendship went back a long way, and when Knight caught up with Parker he learned that he'd angered a man named Juno Eckstrom. Knight was taken prisoner by Eckstrom and put to work in his illegal mining camp. When it all came to a head, Eckstrom and Lee Taylor were dead and Parker and Laramie Calhoun had ridden off for parts unknown. The experience had taken a lot out of Knight. Knight didn't like thinking about the Juno Eckstrom affair because it was such a complicated mess.

"Not much too it. He got blown up and buried in the rubble of his mining operation."

"That's what I heard. What about that snake oil salesman, Jake Grimstone? He rode with a dwarf didn't he?"

"Nicodemus. They died hard. Some men do."

Dobbs nodded knowingly. "You know about Vincent Two Hatchets?"

"I heard."

"He's out here, I can feel it."

"You afraid of him?"

That one had Dobbs smiling. "Can't say that I am but no man wants to die in pain. Bullock said I could stay off the line this time out, but when I heard it was you I changed my mind."

"I hope I can live up to your faith in me."

"The killin's got to be done. The country's getting civilized. We all get paid on time if it's a safe ride."

"You don't think I should take this crazy Indian prisoner if he shows up?"

"Have you given any of the others a chance?"

"I have, but not many."

"Vincent won't give you a chance. He cut off a priest's fingers and butchered a doctor. They say he's as loco as any man can get. Plumb loco."

"I reckon I'll just shoot him then," Knight said sarcastically.

"I reckon you better, because stayin' alive is what I intend. He's got maybe two men with him, Chaska and Wapasha. He robbed the stage twice and he killed the driver Bob Lange who tried to fight. He didn't kill anyone on the second robbery from what I heard. This will be my first meeting with him and I sure hope he's not feeling ornery."

The stage rattled on and Knight watched the trail in

front of them without seeing it, his mind filled with he faces of the dead men he'd killed, although he felt no remorse. What he felt was a resignation, an acceptance that he was riding into battle. He'd been doing it for the most part since the war, and when the fear struck him as it did all men, he allowed his turmoil to become a fury of hatred.

When he simmered down a bit he looked over at Dobbs and asked, "Which one do you think it is? Howell or Reid?"

Dobbs grinned. "I've been pondering that very question. The thing is, I can't figure it. I know one of them is crooked, but I can't place which one. Maybe Reid, but I don't know."

"Could be both?"

"Nope. Too much at stake. One man to take half, let Vincent take the other half."

"Is that what they're saying in the saloons?"

"Half of this haul could make one man set for life."

"It's a mighty heavy strongbox. Big too."

Knight cast a glance over his shoulder at the strongbox. It was old with tarnished brass hinges and worn leather straps over it. He wondered if Dobbs knew it had only rocks in it.

"Howell said he loaded the box himself," Dobbs said.

Knight thought that meant that Reid was in on it. If Howell loaded it with rocks, then Reid thought it was gold. They wouldn't know if the ruse worked until they were ambushed. That's a hell of a circumstance to let happen to capture a robber.

"The woman is a problem, too." Knight said.

"You're dang tootin' she is! There isn't a woman born that doesn't bring trouble. I say they all get branded with a big T for trouble on their ass!"

The landscape grew ugly and the forbidding hills

loomed closer. There was a switching station at Mule Creek and Dobbs said Alistair Devine was getting on in years and might sell out. The old man had survived Indian attacks, outlaws, and the ghosts of pioneers that he said roamed the old wagon trails at night. After the switching station they were in the Cemetery Hills and they should expect to be ambushed.

The sky had filled with gray clouds and Knight could smell the rain coming. He estimated they'd be at the station just about the time the sky opened up. It would be hard traveling so he made up his mind to remain at the station until the rain stopped.

The Mule Creek Station was a ranch house, corral and barn. They pulled up and Alistair Devine came out and waved. He had a long mane of white hair and craggy features with piercing eyes that reminded Knight of an old painting he'd seen of Andrew Jackson. He wore a plain cotton shirt with the sleeves rolled up, stained brown trousers and laced up boots like the ones some drovers wore.

Knight climbed down from the coach still holding the shotgun. He went around as Dobbs huffed out of his seat.

"You sonsofbitches got here just before the storm." Devine said.

Darla, who was being helped out of the coach by Howell, heard Devine and said, "Gracious me! What kind of welcome is that?"

Devine flinched, his face reddening. "Sorry, ma'am, I haven't seen a woman get off this stage in years. This isn't exactly San Francisco."

"No, it certainly isn't," Darla said petulantly as she looked about.

"I've got coffee, eggs and biscuits," Devine was flustered. Darla went inside with Howell and Reid and

51

Devine looked at Dobbs and Knight.

"A lady? In this country?"

"She isn't exactly a lady," Dobbs said.

"She looked like a woman to me!"

"A woman, but not a lady. Hell, Alistair, you want me to spell it out? She knows what a bull needs when its horn is up."

Devine scratched at his whiskered face. "Well, that's fine then."

Knight said, "Let's get these horses in the barn."

One they had unsaddled the horses and put them in stalls with fresh hay, Devine said "You need to have a sentry. There's a bad group riding the trails and if they stop here we're in trouble."

"Vincent Two Hatchets?"

Devine looked perplexed. "Hell, no. That crazy bastard hasn't been seen around here. I was referring to Nick Sandoval. He's out of Yuma after ten years and got himself a gang together. Alex Breen, Lew Porfilo, and Cal Vale."

Knight was flummoxed. He hadn't seen any Wanted papers on those names and was only vaguely familiar with Sandoval's reputation. He was a bank robber but wasn't known to have killed anyone. The last Knight had heard, Sandoval was still in prison although that had obviously changed. The other names were all strangers to him. "What the hell? Where did you hear this?"

"Wells Fargo dispatch came with the last mail box old Dobbs here delivered himself not a month ago. Sandoval has taken to robbing stagecoaches."

Knight spat and rubbed his jaw. "And here I was thinking Vincent Two Hatchets was our biggest problem."

Devine's eyes went wide. "He sure as hell is your biggest problem if he's this far south of Deadwood! That crazy Indian is a killer! Did you hear what he did to that doctor?"

"Yeah," Knight drawled, "and a priest as well. Chopped off his fingers."

"I've been sleeping with my shotgun worrying about Sandoval and now you tell me to worry about an Indian who likes to chop up white men. I'm thinking now that retirement and moving on is about my only choice!"

They walked out of the barn and Dobbs cast a wary gaze at the sinking sun and darkening hills. "Spooks ride those hills and there are canyons and arroyos that can hide an army."

"Stop trying to cheer me up," Knight said, "Let's get some grub."

Alistair Devine made certain that Darla had all she could eat. There were flapjacks and beans, bread, coffee, scrambled eggs, and fresh bacon from a hog Devine said he'd killed a week ago. Richard Howell and Herbert Reid sat on each side of Darla competing for her attention. Reid was telling Darla not to worry about Indian attacks because they were all man enough to keep her safe, and Howell snorted, saying, "At least most of us are man enough to protect you." He tossed Knight a hateful look when he said it.

Two days out of Deadwood and already Knight had one man that would back-shoot him if the opportunity presented itself. Knight's own mood had turned foul after learning that Nick Sandoval was out of Yuma Prison and had started robbing stagecoaches. What were the odds that Sandoval was in the area by coincidence? The entire set-up stunk and he was regretting doing this favor for Seth Bullock. He had the feeling that too many people knew there was a gold shipment on the stage, even though there wasn't one. Of course, it was necessary to bait the hook.

53

That was the whole idea.

Devine made a show of announcing that Darla could sleep in his room and promised to throw a clean blanket on the bed before she retired. To her credit, Darla put on airs of acting like a proper lady and expressed her thanks. Knight decided she would do well no matter where she ended up, but right now his main concern was keeping them from all being killed.

"We need to bring the strongbox in off the stage," Howell announced. Knight told Reid and Dobbs to help him and they all trudged outside. Dobbs climbed up and lifted the box, grunting as he did so, and Howell came up on the seat next to him and grabbed one end. Reid helped carry it down and when they set it down they all had to catch their breath.

"Damn thing is heavy," Dobbs complained.

"Gold is like that," Howell said with a smirk. "It's heavy and it's pretty."

They took the strongbox inside and placed it on the table.

"I'll need coffee in the morning before lifting that again," Dobbs said.

Devine watched all of this with interest. "Four men to protect a chest of gold? Are you ready if anyone makes a play for it?"

"Someone will," Knight said, "I can guarantee that."

"But are you ready? Sandoval has been seen near Laramie and I'll bet he's come north to look things over."

"Who's Sandoval?" Howell asked.

"Robber recently finished his term in Yuma. He's out robbing stagecoaches." Knight said.

"That's the first I've heard of this," Howell said angrily. "As a lawman your responsibility is to keep the Homestake Mining Company appraised of any

54

eventualities. That was guaranteed by Bullock. Now you tell us there's a robber in the vicinity besides Vincent Two Hatchets?"

"Mister Devine mentioned it earlier. That's the first I heard of it."

"How much gold are you boys carrying in that box?" Devine's eyes had a merry shine that Knight didn't like.

"Right about five thousand dollars' worth," Howell said.

Devine whistled. "And four men to get it to Cheyenne?" He laughed. "Vincent Two Hatchets by himself is enough to worry over, but now I heard Sandoval is hunting fast cash. Marshal, I wouldn't gamble on you boys getting as far as Bear Claw Canyon."

"We'll manage."

Devine told them before they get to Bear Claw Canyon there are some rocky outcroppings near the old Oregon Pioneer Trail. "Avoid the older trails. You'll see the markings but some of those switchbacks and canyons are too dangerous for a stagecoach and a six-horse team."

"That might be about where Vincent Two Hatchets is waiting for us."

"Most likely. Getting past the North Platte River won't be easy."

Knight was watching Reid. He hadn't said anything and he was nervously smoking. Reid and Howell both knew the risk when they agreed to ride along. Even if Reid had known there was only rocks in the strongbox, they were aware that coming under attack by Vincent Two Hatchets was a dangerous proposition. It was Seth Bullock who had convinced them that Knight would handle the situation.

Darla was well aware that her presence added a level of excitement for the men, especially Reid and Howell. Knight could see the approval in her eyes as they fawned over her, making a point of getting her coffee, asking if she needed anything. She generated a sexual tension and they all felt it. Reid was the boldest, but it was a façade of gentlemanly politeness he was putting on to impress her. Knight wished they would all shut-up. Their ceaseless small talk was pretentious. Reid was telling her how nice it was to shop in San Francisco, as if he knew everything a woman might want to buy. Darla surely knew that he was a braggart, but she offered wide eyes and placating murmurs of delight. The quick meal couldn't end fast enough for Knight.

Darla retreated to her room and Howell and Reid occupied the two cots off to the side for which Devine charged them a dollar each. Dobbs and Devine made pallets from Mexican blankets on the floor and Knight told Reid he'd take the first watch and wake him at midnight. Knight put an oil lamp on the table next to the strongbox but he twisted the wick low. He only wanted enough light to see when he came in.

He found a spot outside the barn near the empty corral. The night wind blew soft against his chiseled features. The rusted hinge of the barn door creaked ominously in the breeze so he went and closed it. There was no moon but the sky was awash with stars. The dark hills blended into the landscape and all he saw was a darkness that must surely rival the blackness in men's hearts.

He had taken his rifle with him and propped it against the lodgepole fence. His holstered Colt was loaded with five cartridges. The truth was, Knight wasn't expecting trouble. He was taking precautions because his experiences had taught him to take precautions. He didn't like leaving anything to chance.

So far only Howell had given him any trouble, and Knight decided the man's pride was hurt more than anything else. He'd made a mistake and Knight embarrassed him. But he wouldn't make that mistake again. Reid, the banker, had to be in on it with Vincent Two Hatchets. There was no other way for the Indian to know when the stage line was carrying gold. None of them knew about Cole Tibbs riding their trail. That was an ace card that Knight kept hidden away. Tibbs was capable and he was tough.

The wilderness offered nothing new that evening. A coyote howled and he heard the flapping of wings close by. He thought it might be an owl. He listened for the sound of horses out on the trail but there was nothing.

Everything he had seen at the station was orderly and proper. There was a chicken coop so that Devine had eggs. There were extra horses and they were well-groomed and well fed. There was fire wood for the pot-bellied stove and a water pump that brought up clear cold water. With a modest re-supply of certain materials like flour, coffee and some salted beef, Devine could stay here indefinitely, and apparently had.

He woke Reid at midnight and told him not to smoke and not to fall asleep. Knight gave him his Winchester. Reid took his turn at watch without complaint and Knight laid flat on his back on the blanket with his Colt in his right hand. He fell asleep almost immediately and he dreamed briefly about General Sherman on horseback and silhouetted against the buildings of Atlanta burning against the blackness of a cold November night in Georgia. The fires reflected in Sherman's dark eyes; flickering yellow flames danced wickedly in the cavernous pits of darkness.

Knight was awake when Reid woke Howell at three a.m. Howell rose a bit slowly but he also took his turn at watch without complaining. Knight didn't sleep after that. His mind wandered and he dozed a bit, but mostly he was awake and listening. When the rooster crowed he was already up and outside talking with Howell.

"There was nothing," Howell said, "Nothing stirred."

"You can try to sleep in the coach today."

"Do you think this Sandoval is after the gold? Everybody in the damn territory knows that you're here, and they know we're all ready for a gunfight."

"I expect we'll find out today."

Howell went inside to get coffee and Knight looked out over the ridgelines, hills and distant trees. There could be a hundred men out there at that moment, or none.

The hills were beginning to lighten but nothing moved. Knight felt the tension rippling in his back and across his shoulders.

Everybody in the damn territory knows that you're here, and they know we're all ready for a gunfight.

And that was what Seth Bullock had planned. Put the word out, see who shows up. Knight had been a target before, and if he lived through this he'd be a target again. There were a lot of dead men on his back-trail. This entire set-up had been created because Bullock believed that either someone at the bank or someone at the Homestake Mining Company was complicit with Vincent Two Hatchets in the robberies. It was an inside job.

Knight was the perfect man for the job because he didn't care about living, although Bullock had said it with a diplomatic flair. "You're fearless, Max. One lawman and a driver on the stage guarding that much gold is something no outlaw can resist. They'll come gunning for you."

"So you're betting I can handle this without getting killed?"

"Yeah, and I think you'll enjoy it. I think you'll enjoy dropping the hammer on any damn fool that tries to rob that stage."

Knight wouldn't admit it, but Bullock was right. He harbored no sympathy for outlaws. Putting them in a cell and feeding them was a waste of effort. Most of the men he'd killed belonged in a shallow grave; not too deep because he liked the idea of the wolves scavenging the bodies.

There was just enough light to see by and so he made a trek all around the cabin and barn, but there was nothing. When he came around to the porch Devine had come outside with a cup of coffee for him.

"Darla's wearing a tight blue dress. She must think this is a fancy socialite's dance."

"She's got the attention of two men with money. I think she's happy."

"It could be an interesting ride to the station at Bear Claw Canyon."

"Who's the station man?"

"It's more of an outpost. Ernie McGruder runs it. There are no horses. You'll have to rest up rather than switch the team. Ernie is an old mountain man so you can expect bear meat or elk in his stew."

"That will put us less than halfway to Cheyenne."

"Or halfway to hell, depending and on who gets you in their gunsights."

"I expect the trouble will happen before we meet Ernie McGruder."

"Shore it will, and I'm thinkin' about packin' up. I think this country is getting a bit crowded."

Knight chuckled. "There's not a damn soul to be seen in any direction except us."

"Well, maybe I'll see you again and maybe I won't."

Knight sipped the coffee Devine had brought him. It was dark and strong. Devine went to the chicken coop and fetched fresh eggs and went inside to cook. Knight drank his coffee and watched the hills lighten.

Knight had a quick breakfast of eggs and flapjacks and another cup of coffee. As he expected, Howell and Reid sat on either side of Darla who looked pleased with herself. There was little talk, however, except Buster Dobbs was in a jocular mood.

"I slept like a lamb," he said proudly. "Should be a good day for traveling."

They went out and switched the horses and when it was time Knight told Howell, Reid and Darla to get off their asses and get inside the stagecoach.

"Are you always so unfriendly?" Darla asked.

"You should expect we'll all be in danger today. If you're lucky the Indians won't get you. If you're not lucky they'll rape you before they kill you."

Darla's face turned white.

Reid protested, "Now see here, marshal, do you have to scare the poor woman? We'll protect her. You know that!"

"Thank you, mister Reid. I know I can depend on you." Darla looked stricken, but Knight wasn't offering any sympathy this morning.

"You damn fools try and stay alive. Let's go."

Dobbs was whistling "The Battle Hymn of the Republic" as he climbed onto the stage. Darla gave Knight a stern look as she pulled up her skirt and let Reid help her into the stagecoach. Two days out of Deadwood, Knight thought, and I've got a whore and two crooked businessmen to babysit. That was how they left the Mule Creek Station as the sun was rising over the plains of wildflowers and tall-grass pilgrim trails, on a morning that would become blistering hot as they followed the wagon tracks of lost immigrants into the rolling hills and forests of the southern Wyoming Territory which Maxfield Knight knew was about to become a battlefield.

Chapter 6

Cole Tibbs had begun to wonder if he'd ever get married. His fiancé, Jamie Hart, wanted to move east to St. Louis. She wanted to get away from all the dust and rattlesnakes and outlaws. Jamie was still back home in Raven Flats and she's made it clear that it was time he set aside his work as a Deputy U. S. Marshal for a safer occupation. She didn't much care for Maxfield Knight, and it wasn't that long since Knight had come to Raven Flats where Tibbs and Knight had faced off against Carleton Usher and his sons at Snakebite Creek.

The dime novelists still wrote about that showdown, and since then Tibbs had just about had his own bacon fried in several other events, not the least of which being his current situation. Two Indians had been following him for some time; both young, buckskin clad braves, each carrying a rifle. They rode skewbald mustangs and possessed the ability to disappear without leaving a trace, only to reappear like silent apparitions. It was unnerving.

He took to finding deep places in the forest away from any animal trails, and it was here that he slept. But sleeping knowing that two capable and unfriendly Sioux were hunting him made for a restless night. At midnight, when the breeze picked up on that third night, the swirling air made the leaves whisper and he thought he heard chanting in the distance. Maybe it was just nerves. Maybe it was those two buckskin clad Indians chanting some old Indian dirge about taking his scalp. He had his horse hobbled nearby and his horse was restless. That was a bad sign.

Tibbs had his saddle and blanket to prop against with

61

a gun in his hand but sleep was impossible. How did those two Indians know to follow him? Knight hadn't told anybody that he had contacted Tibbs. Somebody had to have been watching Knight when he sent the telegraph and perhaps they coerced the telegraph operator into revealing the contents of the message.

Hell, it didn't matter. They were after him and neither Tibbs nor Knight believed in coincidence. Sure, it was an inside job. Knight's telegraph had been simple. "Follow me from Deadwood. Bullock has sealed letter." That letter which Seth Bullock had given Tibbs twenty-four hours after Knight rode the stagecoach out of Deadwood, outlined all of the details of the robberies, which Bullock himself confirmed on the spot. It was an inside job and a baited set-up to flush out the robber, namely Vincent Two Hatchets.

Tibbs never said anything to Bullock, but he thought Knight was taking a dangerous chance. Knight was sometimes reckless and on more than one occasion Tibbs wondered if the famed lawman had a death wish. Tibbs thought he could ride Knight's backtrail but remain close enough to spot anyone else that might be following. Instead of observing Vincent Two Hatchets following Knight, he'd discovered that he was the one being followed.

The morning broke fresh and clear and the forest was noisy with birdsongs. He ate some biscuits and washed them down with water from his canteen. He wanted coffee but he decided against making a fire. He saddled his horse but led it by the reins onto a deer trail moving uphill. He was in no hurry to ride an open trail.

He went through a cluster of birch trees and then downhill where he heard the sound of water rushing over rocks. The creek was shallow, less than eight feet wide. The water was ice cold and he continued leading his horse along the shoreline, moving south. It was unlikely that his followers knew his precise location, but then again Indians had a way of surprising their enemies. Tibbs was alert to any revealing sounds, but all he heard were birds, the rush of water, and the snorting of his own horse.

He continued in this manner for an hour before pulling himself into the saddle. He wasn't sure of his exact location himself and Tibbs was conscious of the fact that Knight was depending on him. His destination was Mule Creek Station where Alistair Devine could update him on Knight's activities. Yesterday he'd estimated he was forty miles from the station.

The main old wagon route, which had once been a Pony Express trail, was a few miles on his left, clear of the woodland. Tibbs wanted to edge closer to the tree line for a surveillance of the area. If he was lucky he'd spot those two Indians before they saw him.

Tibbs crossed from the trees and onto the rolling grasslands but keeping the forest on his right. His roan picked her way through the sagebrush and wheat fields, skirting a rocky series of connecting hillocks. He saw no sign of life except for some pheasants that he'd spooked and several hawks circling in the sky. The High Plains of the eastern Wyoming Territory appealed to Tibbs. He loved the rugged beauty of the hills and the purple line of mountains visible in the northwest. This was good land for farming but its remoteness and the constant threat of Indian attacks was enough to convince pilgrim families to either turn back or press on to California.

Cheyenne to Laramie was about fifty miles apart but those lonely trails in between were marked with dozens of forgotten graves. The railroad would help civilize this part of the West in the coming years, but the Union Pacific's reputation at creating a "Hell on Wheels Tent City" in Laramie had only slightly improved since the UP put tracks down back in '68. Tibbs had been to Laramie and liked the town, and he respected their law officers, but Cheyenne and Laramie were not the types of wild and woolly towns that Jamie would want to raise their children. Tibbs would have to have some heart-to-heart discussions with his future wife in the months to come.

About an hour later he saw dust at the skyline in front of him. He reined his horse and set his gaze on the distant ridgelines as he swiveled in the saddle and stared off at the hills. A few minutes later he saw four riders crossing from his right to left about two miles ahead of him. He could make out their Stetsons so at least they weren't Sioux. Still, this was remote country, barren of many ranches and home to more than a few outlaws. What men traveled here were often unfriendly, sometimes murderous.

The riders were heading south toward Mule Creek Station which meant that encountering them might be unavoidable. It was crucial that Tibbs get a report from the Station Master, Alistair Devine. There was nothing to do about it. He would let them reach the station first and then ride in about an hour later. He would hold back and hope they didn't notice him on their back trail.

The four riders seemed oblivious of his presence. There was never a time when they appeared to stop and look about. Anyone might be following these fools and they wouldn't know it. That meant they were either stupid or over confident. Given that this was Indian country and the Indians were seldom friendly toward any white man, these four men struck Tibbs as damn fools. But he also wondered at his own judgment, for here he was riding to assist Maxfield Knight on a legal errand that surely appeared foolhardy to most rational men.

The pace was too slow. Tibbs felt hindered by having to keep out of sight while these four strangers rode toward

Mule Creek Station. When the forest thinned out he ventured to ride inside the tree line so he could close the gap and get a better look at these men. What he saw didn't inspire him. Using his father's old army spyglass, he saw four slender and filthy looking drifters in cowpuncher's garb of a vest and shirt, brown slacks and rawhide boots with spurs jangling. They were unshaven and probably stunk to high-heaven. They had been riding a long time and looked done in. Their horses needed rest, water and food. All four men wore gunbelts and had rifles in their saddle scabbards.

Tibbs estimated they would reach Mule Creek Station at twilight. He didn't like it but he might wait and ride in the following morning. The afternoon slipped away and when they were only a few miles from the station Tibbs spurred his horse over a ridgeline, cantering east to find a place to camp. Just as the light was fading, he found a cliffside overhang well off the trail. He hobbled his horse and pulled the saddle off and let his horse to graze amongst the sage and wild grass. He was about to make a small fire when he noticed the cliff walls had been painted and carved with strange symbols. There were handprints on the stone. He recognized a horse and a buffalo and stick figures of the tribe that had lived here in a time so old he couldn't fathom the age of the pictures.

Tibbs wasn't normally superstitious, but those Sioux braves were still out there, and although he hadn't seen them all day, his instincts told him they were still following him. He decided to have a cold camp and satisfied himself with hard tack and water from his canteen. He put his saddle and blanket under the overhanging ridge and slept under the ancient symbols of a buffalo hunt. It wasn't a restful sleep. The wooded hills were alive with animal sounds and his mind had trouble keeping focused. A some

65

point he thought he heard a gunshot but it might have been the crack of a branch snapping under the weight of a passing animal. His eyes flicked open and all he could see were whirls of stars in the heavens.

He was awake as a feeble light began to glow in the east and the outline of hills became visible to his eyes. He could see the contours of the forest as the world brightened. He saddled his horse and set out for Mule Creek Station. If he was lucky those other riders would be gone.

He knew something was wrong when he approached the station. There was no smoke coming from the chimney and he didn't hear the sound of any roosters or chickens, a primary source of food in such a remote location. The corral was empty. Tibbs rode in and called out, "Yip ho, Alistair!" No answer.

He dismounted and pulled his Colt, thumb on the hammer. He swung into the cabin but it was empty. The kitchen utensils and food supplies had been ransacked. He stomped out and approached the barn.

Alistair Devine was on the ground with his head shattered by a .44 slug, his brains blown across the dirt like chunks of red cabbage. One glassy eye reflected the dim light as the barn door swung open. Flies were already buzzing around the body. The horses were gone. Tibbs checked the stalls to be certain the barn was empty, and then he holstered his Colt.

He said "Goddamn it!"

He walked out to his horse and took it to the water trough while he considered his next move. They had taken the stagecoach horses switched out by Dobbs and Knight which made sense considering the poor condition of their own mounts. But where had their horses gone?

He pulled his rifle from the scabbard as his horse drank. He walked around the barn looking for tracks. He found nothing so he went around the station cabin and saw where the horses had left droppings before meandering off.

He cast his gaze across the tall-grass plain and up a short ridgeline where a row of pines pierced the morning sky. The two Sioux bucks sat astride their horses watching him. Four ragged looking horses were nibbling at the grass on the hillside below them.

For whatever reason, those two Indians were following him but had yet to demonstrate any aggression. That could change at any time. They showed no interest in the horses left behind by the four riders.

Tibbs went inside the cabin and picked up several blankets and took them to the barn where he wrapped Devine's body. There was no time to dig a proper grave. He pulled Devine's body into a horse stall and then went out, shutting the barn door behind him. He'd report the murder when he could and ask about someone coming out to bury the old man later.

Tibbs mounted his horse. He was facing a long, uncertain day and the idea of getting married and settling down as a farmer was suddenly quite appealing to him.

Chapter 7

The sky was blue and streaked with small clouds. The landscape seemed to rise up to greet them, and they found themselves first rattling along a bright woodland, and then into a canyon where the rattling and shaking of the harness lines echoed dully off the canyon walls. Plenty of places for an ambush. Plenty of isolated forest trails to hide killers who avoided the sunlight.

It was good they had fresh horses from Mule Creek Station. It was hard going. The horses whinnied, snarled, clomped and neighed their way along the twisting, unfriendly terrain; and all the while Buster Dobbs kept at the whip, cracking it, lashing them, and snapping the leather so that it sounded like gunshots were exploding over the horse's heads.

At ten o'clock that morning they came across horse droppings on the trail. Knight instructed Dobbs to stop. Reid stuck his head out the coach window and demanded to know why they were stopping.

"Stretch your legs," was all that Knight said.

"Remember, marshal, we're armed and can help if necessary."

"Thank you, mister Reid. We'll look around a bit."

Reid was the weakest of the group, and Knight had found most bankers to be short on guts. It was vanity that had brought him on this ride, a way to prove himself. Knight hoped he wouldn't run when the shooting started.

Darla climbed out of the stagecoach making a fuss about getting her skirt dirty. "I may have to let go some water," she said, "and there is little privacy here."

Knight asked Reid and Howell to make certain there were no rattlesnakes on the opposite side of the stagecoach and once they confirmed it Knight said, "Go on the other side."

Darla took care of herself and afterward he followed Dobbs to the horse apples they'd seen on the trail.

"Three, four hours old." Dobbs said.

"Wagon tracks. A heavy wagon, too."

"Conestoga. Yep, big and heavy. The only place they can be going is the outpost at Bear Claw Canyon."

"How did we miss this earlier?" Knight asked.

Dobbs rubbed his whiskered jaw. "We didn't. This wagon crossed from the east. Could be an outpost supplier or a surveyor for the railroad."

The terrain was such that several trails forking south

had merged in the area and they surmised the wagon had come out of northern Nebraska and merged with a southern trail. The wagon was heading toward the outpost at Bear Claw Canyon.

They continued on their way but at a slower pace, partly because the trail was rocky which put extra strain on the horses. Dobbs had gone silent, squinting at the trees and surrounding hills with a wary eye. Knight knew what he was thinking.

The uncomfortable truth being that Vincent Two Hatchets could begin an attack at any moment, and if he chose to simply start shooting there would be fatalities. Everything that Knight had heard indicated that Vincent Two Hatchets was a ruthless killer.

An hour later they came upon the burned frame of the Conestoga wagon. They smelled the dead horses before they saw the wagon. The four mounts had been shot and the air was filled with the loud buzzing of insects. Dobbs halted thirty yards away. Knight saw a raccoon scamper away but it was the flash of brown fur in the brush that concerned him.

"Wolves," Dobbs said.

Knight jacked a round into his Winchester and jumped off the seat yelling into the coach, "Stay inside! There are wolves here!"

Dobbs stood up but had to stay in the seat. Their horses could smell the corpses and probably the wolves as well. They snorted nervously. He held the reins but watched for movement in the brush.

Knight advanced on the wagon and when he was alongside the moldering horse carcasses, he fired his rifle into the brush to scare off the wolves. He knew they wouldn't retreat for long, but they would hesitate for a while. Wolves, Knight thought, were equally as dangerous as angry Indians.

The wagon had been ransacked. It appeared that someone had been transporting flour, canned goods, linens, and some farming implements which had been left behind. A fair amount of flour and canned items had vanished, leaving only what they couldn't carry which was substantial. This was no Indian attack.

Finding the bodies wasn't difficult. The buzzing of the insects around them led Knight off the road and past the sagebrush where he saw the wolf ravaged remains of at least three bodies. The bodies weren't visible from the road, and there wasn't much left. A hungry wolf pack will gorge itself.

Later, Knight thought, a burial party might gather in town and come to help give these poor souls a decent resting place, but that would have to wait.

By the time he had circled the wagon and decided the ambushers were long gone, the sky had turned gray and Knight smelled rain in the air. Howell stuck his head out the coach window and demanded to know what was happening.

"Someone got ambushed," Knight said sharply. "We need to keep moving."

Dobbs spat a thick stream of tobacco juice into the dirt and snapped his whip as Knight climbed into his seat. Once they passed the wagon Knight craned his neck and glanced back to see a wolf already slinking out of the brush to feed on the dead horses.

The hard-packed dirt road was littered with so many small boulders that Dobbs feared they'd crack a wheel if they hit one so he attempted to maneuver the coach around the visible boulders but it was impossible to avoid them all. They were reduced to a snail's pace.

They hadn't gone but a mile when the landscape became steep, the road veering sharply up and to their right, a thick line of pine trees crowding them on each side.

They were confronted by a large pine that had crashed onto the road, blocking their path.

Dobbs cursed and pulled in the reins bringing the stressed horses to a halt. Knight, immediately sensing an ambush, again leaped from his seat with his rifle in hand. Crouching low he advanced alongside the sweating horses, his gaze taking in every tree as he watched for movement.

The minutes ticked away but nothing happened. Then he heard *Whump! Whump!* And he turned in time to see a tree on the road behind them cracking loose and toppling to bar their way. They had been effectively blocked from advancing or retreating.

"Jesus have mercy!" Dobbs bellowed.

Howell screamed from the coach, "What the hell is going on, marshal?!"

There was a span of about a minute when they all held their breath and then a voice boomed from the forest about thirty feet behind them: "All we want is the gold! Nobody gets hurt if we get the gold!"

Knight lifted his rifle and fired a shot at the location where he thought the man was hiding. He heard him whoop, "Hot damn! There's no call for that!"

Howell was rasping at Knight in a harsh whisper, "You got us boxed in and ambushed! I say we rush them! We need to kill those men!"

"Shut-up, Howell. Stay in the coach."

The man in the forest was yelling, "Stop shooting! We could have killed you all if we wanted! All we want is the gold! Take the strongbox down and carry it up this way and leave it!"

Howell bellowed from the coach, "Come and get it! We've got you out-gunned!"

Knight thought: not exactly out-gunned, more like

even odds. But they had one advantage, they could surround the coach and open fire guaranteeing most of them would be killed or wounded. There was only one way to prevent that.

Waving Dobbs down from his seat, Knight asked Reid and Howell to get out of the coach. Knight instructed Darla to stay put and keep quiet. Howell and Reid both emerged from the stagecoach with guns. Howell had his Colt six-shooter but Reid had a small silver derringer in his hand. Knight figured Reid wouldn't be much use, but you know.

Knight explained that if those men surrounded them on each side they would be finished, and to prevent that Knight was going into the forest. He had to be hidden in order to keep an eye on the area surrounding the stagecoach. Glancing at the sky, he also told them a storm was coming. "It's gonna rain like hell. Keep Darla in the coach. Buster, the horses are going to get the worst of it. You need to watch both sides of the coach and try and keep those horses calm."

Dobbs grunted. "I've been in storms before. It'll be hard but we'll get through it."

"You think you can pull this off, marshal? So far you've made a mess of it."

Knight leveled his gaze at Howell. "The U.S. Marshal's office wants to keep the stage line to Cheyenne open. That's my job."

Knight was disgruntled when he slipped into the woods. He felt uncommonly distracted and angered they had been boxed in so easily. He had found a position uphill from the stagecoach where he was partially shielded by the brush but from where he could still see the road. It was a good place of concealment but did him no good when the sky opened up and unleashed a torrent of rain.

He sat there being cold, wet and miserable with a rifle in his hand and nobody to shoot at. He was in a grove of ancient oaks and partially shielded by a canopy of leaves, but as the torrent increased he was buffeted by the rain. He realized he was probably on a fool's errand; no killer would approach them during the storm. Knight couldn't see the stagecoach any longer because the furious rain and mist obscured his view. All the same, it was his job, and that was all he had. He wore the star of a lawman. He concentrated on waiting although his mind flashed back to the farmland of his youth where the purple and yellow wildflowers bent toward the summer sun like old women in church trying to hear the preacher.

Nothing would come of this but death. Maybe it would be his time. Maybe. He thought about Vincent Two Hatchets. What he had heard was motivation enough for Vincent to ride the vengeance trail; to hunt, to torture, to kill. Hadn't Knight himself done the same thing?

There had been a brief time when he was new to the marshal's job that he took some prisoners. Some men were convicted and went to the territorial prison. Every once in a while some paroled robber would come gunning for him, and Knight's trail was marked by many graves. The cold made him shiver and he felt foolish. He thought he was getting old and maybe he wasn't as fast with a gun as he once was.

He gnashed his teeth. He was convinced that Richard Howell of the Homestake Mining Company was complicit with Vincent Two Hatchets. At some point he'd prove it. The way he'd figured it, he'd kill the Indian first, and then Howell might panic and draw on him. All for a chest of rocks?

The wind picked up. He thought he heard rustling nearby but all he saw was a raccoon scampering away. All living creatures faced the same dilemma – to survive. Was God merciless? He often wondered at the reason for it all. Everything he had loved had been taken from him, and all he had left was his gun. What purpose, Oh Lord, is my talent for killing? Does my wife's spirit rest at peace in thy comforting arms? The wind answered his thoughts with a gust of cold, hard rain and the storm rumbled in the sky like the chattering moans of a gut shot man dying in the hills.

The rain had lessened but some time passed before he noticed. Knight was exhausted and when his mind latched onto the fact that the rain had become a drizzle he felt a sense of relief. Knight went down the hill and found Dobbs talking soothingly to the horses. Dobbs was soaked like Knight but he wouldn't complain. "I needed a bath anyway," he said.

Howell and Reid looked worn down; they appeared less professional with the concern and exhaustion showing on their faces. Their neatly cleaned and pressed slacks and coats looked in need of a scrubbing. Darla looked less bright and certainly less demure, even though some of her feminine airs were a façade. Her carefully combed hair was drooping, and her dress was wrinkled. All of them had dried mud on their boots and shoes. Darla looked ready to cry.

None of them were in the mood to talk which Knight was grateful for. He didn't need to listen to their ceaseless prattling and complaining.

His eyes were sweeping the trees looking for movement when a voice called out: "Hello the camp!"

Knight pinpointed the voice's location, his rifle at the ready.

"Hello the camp!"

"I hear you!" Knight called back.

"I propose a truce! Don't shoot! I can help you move that tree!"

"You must be Nick Sandoval."

There was a long pause before Sandoval answered. "That's right. I ain't done nothin' wrong! I was riding with my friends when we got ambushed by Indians!"

"Step out into the road with your hands up."

"I ain't giving up my gun!"

"Step out into the road."

Branches twisted and spurs jangled as Sandoval pushed his way out of clump of brush, his hands held out pleadingly. His gun was holstered.

"Don't shoot!" he said. His voice was stressed.

"Where's your pals?"

"Don't know! We got attacked. I think they was captured by Indians. They came at us awful quick!"

Sandoval had the lean features of a man that hadn't been fed well; there was a pallor to his skin that Knight recognized in men that had been in prison. His unshaven chin was streaked with gray. His eyes gave away his nervousness. They flicked back and forth, taking everything in.

"You're after the strongbox. Give up that idea."

"You got it wrong, marshal. I'm just trying to stay alive."

Knight walked toward Sandoval, careful to keep the rifle in his hand held low. Sandoval didn't back up but he waved his hands and said, "We can work together, marshal! Those Indians mean business! You've gotta let me join up with you! I ain't out to rob anyone or hurt anyone!"

Knight frowned, nodded his head, and then he deftly put the rifle barrel on Sandoval's chest. "Drop your gunbelt! Slow!"

"You can't arrest me, marshal! I ain't done nothin' wrong!"

"I'm not arresting you. I'm taking your gun. You're

going to help us move that tree."

Knight prodded Sandoval with the Winchester's barrel. Sandoval unbuckled his gunbelt and let it fall at his feet. Knight called over his shoulder, "Howell, come on over here and pick up his gun. Sandoval, where's your horse?"

"Back up that hill where I came from."

"Howell, you and Dobbs see if you can find his horse and bring it here. Wear his gun."

"Sure, marshal. We can hogtie this ruffian if you wish."

"We need his horse first. Sandoval, if they don't find your horse or if we get shot at by your friends you'll find yourself gut shot and dying right here in the road."

Sandoval was visibly shaken. "God almighty, marshal. What kind of man are you?"

"The kind that doesn't like ambushers. Get over by the stagecoach."

Dobbs and Howell went up into the trees to find the horse. Sandoval had a glimpse of Darla and Reid in the coach. Knight saw that Sandoval looked up at the strongbox atop the stagecoach, and then into the coach where he appraised Darla.

"This ain't a place for a fancy woman to be traveling."

"She's from Deadwood. There's nothing fancy about her."

Darla, taking offense, said, "You are not a kind man marshal Knight."

"No Darla, I most certainly am not."

"We was going to try prospecting in the Black Hills."

"Was that before or after you took the strongbox off the stage?"

Sandoval looked away, his face red. "Maybe we

76

thought about it marshal, but we haven't done anything against the law. What I said was true. Some Indians attacked us."

"Who was with you?"

"Lew Porfilo, Cal Vale and Alex Breen."

"There was an abandoned wagon. Looked like an ambush. Was that you and your men?"

"No. Honest to God, marshal, we got chased by Indians."

"That was you that cut the tree down."

Knight pushed the rifle barrel into Sandoval's belly.

"Yeah, sure, we did it! It was a mistake! I admit that! It was a mistake!"

Reid, calling out from inside the stagecoach, said, "I'll be glad to teach this fool a lesson, marshal. Just give me the word."

"Let's wait a bit."

Knight felt like walking away from all of them. He was tired and he was soaked. Sandoval looked to be equally done in. They were all frayed at the edges. Only a few days after leaving Deadwood and they were on edge, unhappy and uncertain about what lie before them. Reid looked angry and ruffled.

Knight heard Dobbs and Howell coming down the hill and a horse neighed. They came onto the road and the first thing Knight noticed was the look on Dobbs' face. Dobb tilted his head toward the horse. Knight felt his stomach tighten. He recognized the horse. They'd left it at Mule Creek Station when they switched the team. Knight turned and looked at Sandoval.

"What happened at Mule Creek Station?"

It took a moment. Sandoval had to piece it together. Sandoval's gaze settled on Howell and then Dobbs before it dawned on him. Then he looked at the horse; he looked at the MCS brand plainly visible on its flank, and that's when Knight hit him.

Knight was tall, strong, and he had killed men with his bare hands. It wasn't pride, but it was knowledge of his own strength and the demons that made him pursue killers. Maxfield Knight would always be a man that knew what drove him, and he knew what he was good at. His knuckles turned Sandoval's nose to a splintered, bloody mass of cartilage. The second punch was a sweeping right that slammed into Sandoval's lower-left jaw, breaking teeth and tearing his flesh. He fell gasping, blood pumping from his shattered nose, his mouth an obscene swath of busted teeth. His eyes rolled, blinking rapidly, and then he was wheezing and retching in convulsions.

Howell said: "Jesus, marshal! You don't hold anything back, do you?"

Knight climbed onto the stagecoach and retrieved his satchel which held extra cartridge boxes, gloves, a rain slicker and his handcuff irons which he took and climbed down where he shackled Sandoval's wrists.

Sandoval was trying to breath steadily, the blood still pouring from his destroyed nose. His shirt and vest were stained a deep red. His tears had mixed with the blood on his face and he looked like a gruesome caricature of a man. He was unable to speak. He looked to have bitten his own tongue when Knight hit him, adding more pain to his plight.

"Hurts doesn't it?" Knight asked. Sandoval could only make a whining, blubbering moan. "The way I see it, Sandoval, you don't have to tell me what happened to Alistair Devine. You don't have to say a damn word. Or maybe you'd like to say it was Breen, Porfilo or Vale who did it. Well, it doesn't matter."

Knight was conscious of Darla, Reid and Howell staring at him. Dobbs stood off to the side seemingly unaffected by the violence. "You know why it doesn't matter, Sandoval? Because the truth always comes out. I'll find out what happened to old Alistair. I surely will find out. He was a good man." Knight rubbed his jaw with his callused hand. "Now you're going to help us move that tree." Knight yanked Sandoval by his shirt, forcing him to his feet. "Let's get to work."

It took them the better part of an hour. Sandoval helped tie some chains to the tree and using the Mule Creek Station horse they finally pulled it aside. There was no sympathy for him as he struggled with chained hands, but he did as he was told. There was less than a foot of room but Dobbs was able to maneuver the stage past the downed tree. Knight decided to let the horse go. More than likely the Indians would pick it up. It wouldn't do the horse any good to follow along by a rope. Their horse team was tired and they needed water but they had to press on. Knight believed Sandoval was telling the truth about being attacked by Indians, and that meant Vincent Two Hatchets was nearby.

Knight told Sandoval to get inside the stage. Howell had his guns and Reid would help guard him. Sandoval sat next to Darla who protested, "Marshal! This man smells! You can't expect me to sit here next to him!"

Knight went to the stage door and looked in at Darla. She could not have enjoyed the ice in his eyes as he said, "Not another word, Darla, or I'll leave you here in the road."

Chapter 8

The land was merciless and Maxfield Knight had shown them what that meant as the stagecoach rattled slowly toward Bear Claw Canyon. Over the granite hills and into the deep oaks and pines of a primeval forest. Onward into valleys thick with gnarled brush whose limbs clawed at the sky like skeletal fingers; and then over a ridgeline where all they heard were birdsongs in the trees and the breeze kissed the pines and made a lullaby that was deceptively beautiful in the uncaring glens.

Maxfield's Knight soul was hardened by the long years; it was tested during the war and forged in the fire of his grief after his wife's death. To survive in this land a man had to be tough, he had to react swiftly and if necessary, he had to kill without emotion.

He knew that what he had done to Sandoval had shocked the others. Knight knew that Alistair Devine was probably dead. He knew their situation was going from bad to worse, but he knew what had to be done.

The stagecoach was uncharacteristically quiet as they bumped and lurched along the winding trail. He could see a dark ridge of mossy oaks and tall pines far ahead of them; and on their right it was obvious by the serrated difference in the treetops that they followed a trail that curled into a valley of steep hills. Then Knight saw movement between the trees and he pointed so that Dobbs might see it as well. Neither of the spoke but Dobbs saw what Knight had seen – an Indian on horseback. It might have been a skewbald mustang but as the stagecoach moved forward the Indian was obscured by the trees.

An Indian on a fresh horse. Their team of four horses were tired and they had to find water. Knight was hoping they'd come across a creek. They couldn't push these horses much farther. The storm had frightened them, sapped their energy.

Ten minutes later they came across a hillside with less trees and there sat two Indians astride their horses. When Dobbs and Knight saw them the two bucks yipped and hollered, making derisive whooping calls to show their defiance, but also to show how little they feared them. Knight thought they were also laughing at them.

"Pull 'em up, Buster," Knight said softly.

The stage clattered and squeaked before coming to a halt. This resulted in an explosion of laughter from the two Indians. They raised their lances and shook them, wailing like excited coyotes.

"They're testing us," Dobbs said.

Howell called up from the coach: "What is it, marshal? Is it an Indian attack?"

Knight craned his neck and called down, "Sit tight and don't get out."

The Indians continued laughing at them, their cackling and hooting filling the air. Knight studied them. They had Henry rifles in scabbards but carried only lances.

He had his first look at Vincent Two Hatchets when he noticed movement in a grove of hillside oaks on a steep ridge where the leaves chattered in the breeze like a mocking copy of the Indians laughing at them. At first he thought it was a deer but then the horse came into view and Knight knew without question who it was. Taller than he expected, even on horseback; strong and fierce looking. Intelligence blazed in the man's eyes, and something else; something that made Maxfield Knight believe with certainty that he might not survive this expedition. Defiance; a feral wildness and hatred that came from some dark pool of grief. The marshal knew that look because he saw it in his own eyes when he looked in the mirror when he shaved.

The other two Indians finally drifted out of sight but Vincent Two Hatchets, the Tomahawk Killer, sat astride his horse looking directly at U. S. Marshal Maxfield Knight, studying him. Knight felt an odd combination of

81

apprehension and respect. From everything he'd heard, this man had every reason to wage a war against white men.

Without thinking, Knight raised his hand to acknowledge Vincent Two Hatchets. He didn't know why he did it; maybe an impulse. A gesture of peace between two men who would soon try to kill each other. At the same moment, the Indian's horse shook his head, its mane catching the breeze, and it neighed and clopped his left front hoof. Then Vincent Two Hatchets tugged the reins and turned the horse into a whispering grove of ancient trees that shielded him like a row of sentries.

"What the hell was that?" Dobbs asked.

"We need to keep moving."

Dobbs snapped his whip and the team jolted forward. Howell was calling up from the coach as they lurched forward: "Marshal, what the hell is going on?"

Twisting in his seat, Knight yelled down, "Some hostile Indians. Keep quiet until we stop."

To Knight's relief they were going downhill and a mile later the trail leveled out alongside a running stream. They heard the sound of the water before they saw it. There was a short grassy clearing nearby and Knight ordered Dobbs to pull the stagecoach off the trail. They would have to make a temporary camp, allow the horses to drink and graze.

When they stopped, Knight leapt from the seat and explained to the others what was happening: "These horses need water. We'll stop here but we need to stand ready to fight. There's at least three Indians nearby. So far they haven't attacked, but that could change at any time. Sandoval stays in the coach. Darla, you can stretch you're your legs but stay near the men. Buster and I will unharness the horses and take turns walking each one to the water. Howell, you and Reid stay alert, one of you on each end of the coach."

It was the most he had said at one time to this group and for once there were no questions, no push-back.

Getting the horses unharnessed took some time, but they walked them to the stream and let them drink, and they hobbled them so they could graze in the tall grass. There was no attack, no sign of Vincent Two Hatchets and the other Indians. Knight wondered if this was like a game for them; a lethal game to be sure, but a sporting game. Hunting was like that for some men, a game of skill where anything could happen.

The rumbling of the cold water rushing over the rocks mingled with the sound of birdsongs. The air smelled like pine and the mossy scent of the earth and the water. Knight had led the last horse to the creek for water and then up onto the grass to feed when an arrow sliced through the air and punctured the horse's neck. The animal screeched piteously, rearing up on its hind legs, the bloody arrowhead gleaming crimson in the sun.

In that same instant a flaming arrow came arcing toward them from behind, on the opposite side of the trail, and it slammed into the stagecoach. Howell was screaming and shouting, but there was nothing to shoot at. The Indians were out of sight.

The horse's reins were torn from Knight's hands as the injured horse thrashed wildly. The other horses became agitated by the scent of blood and the dying horse's distress.

Reid had started shooting across the road and Knight had time to bellow, "Save your ammunition! Put out that fire!"

Howell climbed onto the stagecoach and yanked loose the flaming arrow and slapped at the flames before they could take hold. It was impressive at how coolly Howell had acted. Reid, on the other hand, was blasting away like a damn fool. He reminded Knight of a bad actor in one of those Wild West shows the easterners loved so much.

With Indians shooting arrows at them from across the creek and the opposite side of the road, their defensive options were limited.

Blood was dribbling steadily from the horse's wound and Knight realized that pulling the arrow free wouldn't save the animal. With a detachment that he allowed to blossom with a practiced coldness, Knight pulled his Colt and shot the horse in the head. The animal dropped and Knight clenched his teeth. Killing the horse made him angry, but there was no sense in letting the creature suffer.

When he turned around he saw that Buster Dobbs had an arrow in his arm. The old drover grimaced and pulled the arrow out, tossed it away, and then untied his bandanna and began to wrap the wound. Knight went and helped him, tying off the bandanna so it was tight enough to stop the bleeding.

Dobbs looked at the dead horse. "They're gonna pick at us a little bit each day."

"Yeah, they will. We can still move on for Bear Claw Canyon."

Howell came huffing up to Knight, his face sweaty and red. "Marshal, this is out of control! Those Indians will kill us! I say we give them the gold! Isn't that what Vincent Two Hatchets wants?"

"You seem to forget this entire expedition was set-up to bring him to justice."

"And how do you plan on doing that? He must have a dozen Indians with him!"

"No, I think only two."

"How do we survive this? Tell me that!"

Reid came over looking calmer than he should have.

"I'm certain I killed at least two of them. I saw them in the trees."

"You didn't hit anything except bark and leaves." Knight snapped. He lifted his head, turned and looked all around them. The attack had stopped. *It is a goddamn game and I'm losing*, Knight thought, then he growled, "Help me get these three horses reharnessed. We need to keep moving."

"A three-horse team isn't much," Howell said.

"It'll have to do."

Reid looked appropriately chastised but he helped Knight and Howell get the horses ready while Dobbs stood by the stage and informed Sandoval, "I'm looking for a reason to shoot you, so go on and try to escape."

The glowering Sandoval stayed in the coach next to Darla who had turned pale, her lips pressed tightly together. Dobbs thought she looked so scared she might wet herself. Dobbs thought he should say something comforting, but his arm hurt and a good horse had died, so he spit a wad of tobacco juice into the dust and said a silent prayer for their safety, although he wasn't certain if it would help.

Dobbs cracked his whip and the stage lurched forward. Knight had his Winchester across his knees and the shotgun was resting at Dobbs' feet.

"Gonna be a long day," Knight said.

Chapter 9

Deputy U. S. Marshal Cole Tibbs only drank on Christmas and his birthday but with two Indians tracking him he suddenly felt the need for a snort of red-eye whiskey. The rain was hammering him and his horse was frightened. He should have sought shelter among the thick trees but he pressed on from a sense of loyalty to Maxfield

Knight. He heard gunfire far away; a distant echo whose true direction he was unable to determine.

He finally stopped, slipped out of the saddle and led his horse into a gnarled vale of twisted oaks and tall pines. The trees partially shield them from the blistering rain. Dark clouds rose like the ruins of old cathedrals mocking the promise of heaven. Lightning flickered and thunder cackled and he stood shivering with his fatigued horse. A peal of rolling thunder was like a death knell that caused his horse to screech and bolt away, the reins yanked loose from his slicked fingers.

Tibbs tried running after the horse but the steed had swiftly disappeared into the woods, propelled by its own exhaustion and fear. With the horse went his rifle and his saddlebags with a modest supply of hard-tack, biscuits and coffee. The other saddlebag held his extra cartridges. His survival options had been reduced to a Colt holding five rounds and his holster loops with fifteen extra bullets. Tibbs huddled under the trees, sopping wet, cold, and regretting every moment of this ill-fated assignment.

Adding insult to injury was the fact that he had come to realize that he had been skillfully misguide onto an alternate old wagon trail. He realized this cold fact just before the rain hit. There had been no wheel tracks from the stagecoach for several miles. He cursed himself for not noticing it sooner.

He knew how they had fooled him. An Indian had made an appearance in front of him about a half mile ahead, and Tibbs had instinctively taken a trail to the right. He hadn't realized it at the time, but that fork in the road had taken him slightly north, and away from the direction of the Deadwood stagecoach. They were herding him as if he were a stray cow.

He wondered about those two Indians. Tibbs had but

modest experience and little knowledge about Indians. He possessed far more knowledge about outlaws, bank robbers, drovers and cowpunchers, but at the moment such knowledge was useless. He had heard that Indians believed in strange things; that the ghosts of their ancestors haunted these wild Wyoming hills; that the great chiefs could ride the wind, their feathered headdresses adorned with eagle feathers to help them navigate the mountain air, and one day they would lead an army of dead warriors against the blue coats for a final battle. He heard the squaws at the Little Big Horn had butchered the bodies of the 7th Cavalry so that their spirits would suffer in the afterlife. Southern Wyoming, he had been told, was home to deformed Sioux trolls and giants who lived in caves and ambushed wagon trains because they favored the cooked flesh of white people.

No question about it, he needed a drink.

Cole Tibbs was lost, at the mercy of two Indian braves who were probably not yet twenty years old, and who had skillfully led him around a complicated circle.

When the rain finally stopped the fog lay like a fleece across the valley and Tibbs had trouble seeing twenty feet in front of him. He stumbled about longer than he should have looking for his horse. The leaves were heavy from the rain and all about him was the steady dripping of raindrops falling from the trees with each gust of a thick, humid breeze that made it difficult to breathe. Discouraged, he plodded on, occasionally whistling and hoping to find his horse munching at some grass.

As he walked, he thought about his fiancé, and he wondered if she was thinking about him. Tibbs felt that his days as a lawman were coming to an end, and he prayed it wouldn't end with his corpse lying undiscovered in the forest for decades. It was to his credit that he shared with

Maxfield Knight the characteristic of stubbornness. There is something to be said for a man that was too stubborn to quit on any venture that he started. Some innate sense in him; some wisdom born from his experience lent to him a notion that he was going to survive. He owed it to the marshal, and he owed to himself. Getting home to his betrothed, Jamie Hart, was motivation enough. His hometown of Raven Flats was another world away, and the idea of ranching was appealing.

After wandering in a circle for thirty minutes he stopped, sucking in the humid air. He had been cold when the storm hit but now he was exhausted and feeling stifled by the humidity. His wet clothes clung to him like an undertaker's damp blanket. He sat on a fallen tree and rested. His calculating mind assessed his options. He had been going about everything the wrong way. Deviating from the main wagon trail had been a crucial mistake, but returning to it simply put him at the mercy of the Indians again. He guessed they didn't quite know where he was any better than he knew where they were.

The Indians were playing with him, having their sport. That, he decided, was an advantage. They didn't want him dead just yet. He needed a better sense of the landscape. As the fog slowly lifted, his gaze followed the treetops that rose in segregated lines up a steep hill. The curving rows of trees reached an apex on a slope that might have been more mountain than hill. He started up the slope, bushing first through a rocky gorge and then breaking through a wall of underbrush. It was slow and difficult work. Tibbs removed his sopping shirt and tied it around his waist. He was besieged by gnats and mosquitoes but he refused to acknowledge their irritating presence. Steeling himself, he pressed onward, moving methodically but steadily. Sweat dripped from under his Stetson as he huffed, climbed, and sometimes nearly crawled up an impossible hill. His flesh stung from the mosquito bites and sometimes a gnat was sucked into his mouth when he was gasping for breath, forcing him to hack it up and cough.

To survive meant being relentless. He stopped frequently, breathing hard, and when his pulse slowed he pushed on for more ground. It was a meticulous and unpleasant trek up that hill, and when he reached the summit he lay on the ground and watched the gray clouds scurry across the heavens until he saw a patch of blue sky. He felt abandoned, but oddly he didn't feel completely alone. He thought that God was watching him. Maybe this was a test, although why God would test him was unknown. Jamie often told him that the good Lord worked in mysterious ways. He didn't really understand any of that, but Jamie often prayed and asked God to do good things for people. Tibbs thought that sounded a tad selfish, but after being chased by Indians and battered by a violent summer storm he thought it wouldn't hurt to try a prayer, so he asked God to help him find his damn horse.

He heard crows cawing in the forest nearby. Crows, he thought, made those sounds when they were hungry and when they had found food. Possibly there was a dead animal nearby, or possibly they were sizing him up for a feast in the same manner that vultures circled their prey on the high winds.

Turning on his side, Tibbs pushed himself to his knees, rose to his feet and slapped at the mosquitoes on his chest and arms and leaving bloody tattoos across his body. From his position on the hilltop he could only see a green valley that offered little opportunity. He needed to move eastward for a look at the next ridgeline.

He stumbled along a thin animal trail and into an eerie silence that clung to him like a fervent lover. Anger

89

slithered through his muscular body and he forced himself not to quit. He was relieved when he finally reached a point where he had a better view of the land below him. His eyes took everything in slowly and deliberately. The sun glinted off a thin wisp of a stream down in the valley, and he estimated it was due west of the place where his horse had run off. Getting to it meant descending into the sweltering, humid forest.

His eyes were knifed to the path and he walked slowly, conserving as much energy as possible. It took him an hour and a half to reach the stream. He found the water behind a clump of berries and the first thing he saw in the shoreline mud were bear tracks. Tibbs, who enjoyed fishing, thought that under other circumstances this would have been a nice place to throw a line out. He waited to make certain no bears were nearby, and then he stripped and stepped into the cool water.

The first order of business was pulling the ticks off his chest and arms. Then he submerged and reveled in the cool water. The current was steady, still cold from the winter snows, but Tibbs didn't linger. He waded out of the water and let the sun dry him before he dressed. He had just buckled on his gunbelt when he heard a horse whinny. He recognized the sound of his own horse, as any good horseman would.

Tibbs followed the shoreline, the current running smooth and golden over the jumbled rocks. He saw the flashing gills of some fish in a ripple of sunlight. Another half an hour passed but he heard nothing but the wind and the birds.

He was surprised when he eventually came to a curve where the stream was wider and deeper. He found hoofprints. His horse was following the stream south. Tibbs edged through the greenery until he came upon a clearing where he finally saw his horse.

A fierce looking Indian sat astride Tibbs' horse and there was a rage in his eyes that conflicted with the calm manner he held the reins. An Indian came up next to him and put a rifle barrel to his head. Another Indian came up on his left and looked at him without emotion.

The man that he knew with certainty was Vincent Two Hatchets nodded his head. Tibbs didn't have to guess who he was. The two tomahawks in his belt and the fury in his eyes was enough. Tibbs was astounded when the man spoke perfect English.

"My brother with the gun at your head is Wapasha, Red Leaf. Please don't move. Chaska will take your gunbelt."

The Indian came and unbuckled the gunbelt.

"I'm just a traveler," Tibbs said, struggling to think of something that might spare him. "I lost my way."

"You're a damn fool like the marshal. We'll take the gold and maybe torture you before we kill you all. I haven't decided yet."

"How?" Tibbs almost stammered. "How do you know these things?"

"I knew before marshal Knight left Deadwood. Your appearance was told by a telegram he sent. Now follow Chaska. My camp isn't far."

Chapter 10

They arrived at the Indian camp in the late afternoon when the crescent moon was manifesting itself in the turquoise sky; on a day when the milkweed was waist high and the monkshood grew in the moist shade and the red windflowers reminded Tibbs of blood splatters as they settled into a secret glen that he knew he'd never be able to find again.

A man held prisoner and condemned to death is the lowest a man can go. His choices involve deciding if he will crumble, overcome by emotion, weeping and pleading for his life, or of remaining stoic and praying that he can hold onto a small measure of dignity. Tibbs found himself remaining calm. He had, in fact, not given up hope. He was also surprised by the camp's orderliness, its attention to practical comfort. Tibbs remained quiet, watching everything they did to determine if an opportunity for escape might present itself.

The Indians had three prisoners. They were the same men he had seen on the trail although one was missing. Their hands were tied behind their backs with sturdy hemp. Tibbs asked who they were and they told him, Breen, Porfilo and Vale. Their friend Sandoval, the leader, had disappeared when they attacked the stagecoach. They readily admitted to plotting a robbery once they heard the stagecoach was carrying a gold shipment on behalf of the Homestake Mining Company.

"That damn Sandoval talked us into it," Breen said, "I'll kill him if I see him again."

"You backed him faster than I did," Vale said, his eyes blazing from between the greasy locks of his hair that had fallen across his unshaven face. He looked like a wild beast.

Porfilio was the silent one, staring with abject dismay at the Indians, having resigned himself to an early grave.

"Did you see a U. S. Marshal?" Tibbs asked.

"Yeah, down by the stage. They have a woman with them."

"A fine-looking woman," Vale said.

"Sandoval had us block the road by cutting a tree down. That lawman wouldn't give up the gold. Then these

Indians came at us just before that storm hit."

Chaska had collected wood for a fire and had it all arranged but he didn't make a fire. The three prisoners were made to sit together, lined up around a barrier of trees. They left Tibbs alone, although they watched him carefully. He didn't understand why they hadn't tied his hands.

Vincent Two Hatchets observed all of their activities with an unnerving silence. After tethering the horses, he sat on a fallen tree and watched them. Breen, Porfilo and Vale found this disturbing and muttered about it to themselves and avoided eye contact with the Indians. Tibbs realized they must not know that Vincent spoke English.

"He can understand you," Tibbs said.

Vincent laughed dryly; the corners of his mouth pulled back into a faint semblance of a smile. "Yes, I can. These three will die first."

Tibbs locked eyes with Vincent. He wouldn't look away although the savage rages evident in his expression sent a cold chill through him.

"I'm confused," Tibbs said, "An educated man waging a war he can't win. You can kill all of us but more men will come. They won't stop."

"No, they will not stop. I don't expect them to. Joshua fought such a battle as this. He lived to be an old man. The blue coats and farmers will never conquer the wild lands. I can fight and I can hide. Your history tells me this."

"You have read the Bible but you cut up a priest."

"With pleasure. I cut off his fingers and then I killed a physician who refused to help my wife."

"Why do you need gold? Don't you have everything you need to keep killing?"

"Taking the gold is a way to barter. Joshua paid his spies before the conquest of Canaan."

"You're not paying for a war; you're paying men to help you get revenge."

"Is there a difference? Watch carefully, lawman, my battle will succeed."

Vincent nodded once to Wapasha who pulled the deputy's arms behind his back and lashed them with rope that bit into his flesh and nearly cut off Tibbs' circulation. He winced as he was shoved back and forced to sit cross-legged across from the other prisoners.

Twilight came and no one spoke; the forest crackled gently with the movements of small animals and the litanies of birds. The sunlight crashing through the trees seemed like an ancient light that bathed them in a deceptive glow of tranquility. Chaska made a fire when the sky darkened and they existed in a silent circle of blazing embers below a star-packed lavender heaven. They were not given any food or water. The three Indians shared a rabbit they cooked over the fire and they ate it by pulling it apart with their fingers. This, Tibbs thoughts, was a kind of torture. The prisoners were starving and the smell of the cooked rabbit filled the air.

Tibbs saw no indication that this was a regular camp. They made camp on the move, choosing their location carefully. They were hidden, fed, armed and prepared to kill, although Tibbs sensed there was another reason for this cat and mouse game they seemed to be playing.

They hadn't made a move against the stagecoach yet. Only Sandoval's gang had made that attempt, failing miserably. The rope binding his wrists cut into his flesh. Tibbs knew that Knight would be simmering with anger. All that long night Tibbs slept fitfully. Whenever he opened his eyes one of the Indians was awake and staring at him impassively. They possessed a remarkable reserve of energy. Before dawn his eyes fluttered open and Vincent

Two Hatchets was watching him. He seemed almost regal with his cotton shirt and bone necklace, two tomahawks in his belt, the blades catching the waning glow from the dwindling embers.

They were roused at sunrise and each prisoner was untied in order to relieve himself although Porfilo had wet himself in his sleep. This was a source of great amusement to Chaska and Wapasha who cackled gleefully. They all had their hands tied again and they set out walking with the Indian trio following on horseback. They used Tibbs horse as a packhorse although they only had a few canvas sacks of supplies. Vale led the way followed by Breen, Porfilo and Tibbs. Porfilo stank of urine and sweat and marched with his head down, thoroughly humiliated. It was a sullen and oppressive march along winding trails, besieged by insects and apparently walking themselves toward their own demise.

Tibbs decided that killing the three Indians would be a formidable task. Vincent Two Hatchets by himself would be a hard man to kill. Yet thus far the strongest skill they had demonstrated was evasion, followed by the fear generated by the murders Vincent had committed.

The prisoners were exhausted by the time the sky turned pale. They came to the old wagon trail and Tibbs thought this was the route the stagecoach was following. They came to a low place in the road surrounded by thick rows of pines and a stranglehold of wild brush, following it uphill for half a mile before stopping. Vincent was looking back the way they came and Tibbs realized the stagecoach was coming from behind them. He initially thought they were following the stagecoach. Vincent spoke in his own language and Wapasha took Tibbs with Breen and Vale off the road and onto a humped grassy knoll where they could see the road over the clawing brambles and spiked leaves.

95

Porfilo began whimpering. Chaska knocked him to the ground and tied his ankles with a long stretch of rope. Wapasha joined him while they waited on the hillside with Vincent Two Hatchets astride his horse behind them. Tibbs felt anxious and small, helpless in what he thought was going to be an execution, and he wasn't wrong. But they wouldn't kill Porfilo right away. There was another motive to their actions.

Wapasha and Chaska had knotted Porfilo's ankles together, his hands still tied behind his back, and together they found a study tree and looped the rope around a high branch. Together they pulled Porfilo so that he was dangling upside down just to the right. He would be plainly visible to the occupants of the stagecoach when they wheeled down into that low section of road.

Porfilo began weeping. They could hear the wracking sobs and Tibbs had to look away. It was monstrous. He looked at Vincent but the Indian showed no emotion. Their eyes met and he said to Tibbs in a mocking tone, "Praise God indeed."

It wasn't long before they heard the rattling and clopping of the Deadwood stage. Tibbs was surprised to see only three horses. The stage was moving slowly as it began to descend into the low section of road, and Tibbs saw Knight in the shotgun seat next to a grizzled old driver. They stopped the stage when they saw Porfilo hanging upside down from the tree. He heard the driver say, "I think he's still alive."

Tibbs knew that Vincent Two Hatchets would make his move then, and he did swiftly. Chaska put a flaming arrow into Porfilo's belly, igniting his shirt and causing the doomed man to scream in pain. Tibbs turned on Vincent and snapped, "Shoot him! Put him out of his misery!"

"You are too soft for a lawman."

Porfilo burned and bled simultaneously. Tibbs watched in horror as U. S. Marshal Maxfield Knight racked a cartridge into his Winchester's breech, slammed the stock to his shoulder while sighting down the barrel before snapping the trigger. The bullet exploded Porfilo's head, the gore pouring into the road beneath him. The stagecoach was in pandemonium as the passengers frantically piled out.

"God almighty! What have you done, marshal?"

He was the smallest of the men, dressed like a banker. Knight cursed at him and bellowed, "Get back in the goddamn coach you damn fool!"

The woman began screaming. One of the other men slapped her hard across the face, took her roughly by the arm and forced her back into the stagecoach. One of the men was dirty and ragged looking. Tibbs thought that had to be Sandoval who had survived the attack earlier. There was an exchange of harsh threats and confused yelling.

Tibbs was about to call out to Maxfield Knight when Vincent Two Hatchets chose this moment to make his presence known. It had to be a moment that Knight and the others in the stagecoach would never forget, and Tibbs watched with both horror and admiration as the Indian cantered his horse onto the high road near Porfilo's bloody, smoldering corpse. He raised a tomahawk to the sky and barked "Yip-yip-yip!" which to Tibbs sounded like a victory cry.

Chaska and Wapasha had vanished. Tibbs ran toward his horse even though it was futile with his hands tied behind him. His rifle was still in the saddle-boot but there was no way he could use it. He stumbled and fell just as a barrage of gunfire was unleashed from the stage. It was no use, he knew, because Vincent and put his heels to his horse and leapt from the road. Bullets slashed and careened through the woods, chipping uselessly at bark and brush.

Tibbs stumbled to his feet and watched Vincent jump effortlessly from his horse and yank loose the rifle Tibbs had wanted. Glaring at him, Vincent said triumphantly, "With your rifle my vengeance will sting them."

Striding past him without the least bit of concern, Vincent seemed to glide up onto his horse, an unreal and highly skilled combatant; and with a one-handed jerk of the reins he set the horse in motion and raced out to again attack the stagecoach.

The ferocity and brutality had numbed Tibbs. He rolled sideways, and forced himself to his feet. Breen and Vale had fled. His bound wrists ached terribly and he felt the stickiness of blood where the rope had ripped at his flesh. There was a thrumming in his ears, the pounding of his own heart in his chest echoed with the regularity of a metronome. It took him several wild minutes of scrambling about the brush to get his bearings. When he saw Vincent on horseback again he had come downhill near the road. Vincent had fired several shots with the rifle but none of the bullets had struck the stagecoach. Tibbs could plainly see Vincent shoot high, over the coach.

His confusion was replaced with the realization that this was a game for the Indians. From somewhere on the opposite side Chaska and Wapasha unleashed a flurry of flaming arrows, some of which struck the stagecoach again. The woman inside the stagecoach began screaming and Tibbs could hear men cursing.

Tibbs didn't see Knight. He saw an old, bearded stage driver with the brim of his Stetson flattened out raise his shotgun and send a blast toward Vincent Two Hatchets but the Indian had anticipated the shot and reined his horse in a swift, wide circle that reminded Tibbs of the antics of those Wild West performers. They packed tents full of people thrilled to see such horsemanship demonstrated against the attacks of the savage hordes. Tibbs was watching a game of skill where the stakes were a man's life, and on this day Vincent Two Hatchets proved he could escape a shotgun blast at close range with the tug of leather reins and a horse's ability to swiftly move its body as the Indian tilted sideways and bent low against the saddle. The shotgun blast tore into the trees.

The morning tranquility had been shattered, the raindrops clinging to the leaves from the storm were glistening in the trees like diamonds, while behind the stagecoach Tibbs heard men cursing as Chaska and Wapasha taunted them with a reminder at the lethal effectiveness a well-placed arrowhead could have on the human body. Rifles cracked and lead tore through the air, frightening the birds from the branches, flinging the raindrops that still clung to the leaves which dropped on them like warm tears.

The old stagecoach driver dodged out of sight and Vincent Two Hatchets cantered into view. Tibbs was mesmerized. There was something in the Indian's face that Tibbs hadn't seen before; it was an emotion that intermingled with the anger that was ever-present in Vincent's features. It was the physical manifestation of a cruel satisfaction that Vincent took in terrorizing his enemies.

A short, stocky man stumbled into view with an arrow stuck in his shoulder. He yelped in pain as Maxfield Knight stepped from around the stagecoach and yanked the arrow free, a gout of blood darkening his shirt. Vincent Two Hatchets pushed his horse into gallop as he crossed the road, rushing toward Tibbs. The horse's hooves kicking up great clods of moist soil from the rain-soaked earth. The Indian punched his heels into the horse's flanks and the horse obediently nuzzled Tibbs having recognized him, and the deputy fell backward landing on his swollen hands.

Squinting through the pain he saw Vincent Two Hatchets glide from the saddle in a heartbeat, an apparition of strength and dominating power. Vincent smiled. "My name will be known in your newspapers, a killer of Christian men!"

Tibbs was pulled to his feet, grunting in pain. "You're insane!"

Vincent had swung around, sighting the rifle toward the stagecoach, and when he fired Tibbs heard the bullet smack into a horse. The horse dropped without a sound, a fountain of blood splaying from a terrible wound on its head. The other horses panicked, rearing up, but unable to flee with the weight of the dead horse jumbling the harness.

"Do tell me, deputy, how far can that stage go with two exhausted horses?"

Chaska suddenly appeared and took Tibbs roughly by the arm and began leading him through the forest. There was a spattering of gunfire behind them. Tibbs tried to look over his shoulder but Chaska nudged him with the barrel of an old Spencer rifle that Tibbs hadn't seen before. There seemed to be no end to their resourcefulness.

They arrived at the camp and Breen and Vale had been lashed to a tree. Their faces showed their exhaustion and despair. The Indians had anticipated their every move and Tibbs was certain they faced a brutal and painful death. The ropes holding Breen and Vale were so tight they looked as if they could barely breathe. Breen's lips were swollen and one eye was puffy and purple. He had put up a fight and paid a price for it.

Tibbs sat on a log, his bound arms and his shoulders ached. He waited for them to tie him to a tree as they did Breen and Vale but they left him alone. After a few minutes he said to Vincent, "I have to piss."

"Of course you do." Vincent Two Hatchets was licking his fingers after eating another rabbit that Chaska had caught. The Indians hadn't wasted a morsel of the rabbit, sucking at the bones and mashing the cartilage with their molars.

"Won't you allow me some dignity before my death?"

Vincent strode over to Tibbs and violently pulled him off the log, turned him over and with one expert swipe his tomahawk cut Tibbs free. For a moment Tibbs thought the blade had cut into his flesh because he felt a sharp pain, but then he realized it was the pain of the pressure from the ropes being released. He rolled, pushed himself up, his wrists, hands and arms tingling as the circulation began to return. He felt as if he was being stabbed a hundred needles. He rubbed his hands together. He couldn't entirely feel with his fingers.

All three Indians watched him with interest. They appeared to be studying him, almost as if they were curious. Tibbs relieved himself but as he buttoned his trousers he heard horses and he turned his head in time to see several more Indians with horses moving along the trail just behind the camp. More than three, he thought. Goddamn, more than three. He turned around as Vincent Two Hatchets was biting at a morsel of rabbit, his eyes shining with amusement. Before Tibbs could ask about the other Indians, Vincent Two Hatchets wiped his greasy fingers on his buckskin breeches and said, "I wish to know what it's like to be in the Lord's building? Can you tell me what that's like?"

Tibbs was dumbfounded. This was a relentlessly cruel game and he was beaten.

"I'm finished, Vincent. You've won. Kill me and be done with it."

"The implication is that I shall find comfort in God's house, but I have never seen it."

"I am not responsible for your grief."

"Are you afraid to die?"

"Yes."

"You give up so easily. I'm disappointed." Vincent turned his head and examined Breen and Vale. "These two shall feed the wolves."

Vincent Two Hatchets cut Vale loose and he fell to his knees whimpering. Vincent came up behind him and curled his fingers in Vale's hair. In the span of an eyeblink Vincent had swung his tomahawk with such force that Vale's head was decapitated. Vincent deftly stepped back as the body lay quivering, a fountain of blood gushing from the neck, the head swinging and dripping in Vincent's hand. He waited a moment as the blood drained from the head before holding it aloft.

"Here is a creature of God," Vincent Two Hatchets said in a soft, reverential tone, "and may the silence on his lips speak a language that warns my enemies that death follows them, death leads them, and I shall sing a victory song when I kill them!"

Chapter 11

Fire is mesmerizing. It moves intelligently and logically, consuming everything in its path. The burning buildings moan and crackle, making a sound like an old woman on her death bed, fingers twitching, her mouth open as she sucks in the billowing black smoke that will choke the life from her. The fire illuminates the side of the clapboard buildings and the people rushing past throw weirdly long shadows against the walls. An army of grotesque figures march past and the streets of Atlanta reverberate with the sound of anguish. The cool November night was a relief after the warmth and tick-infested camps at Shiloh. When he sleeps, Maxfield Knight often coughs, his throat dry, his hands clenched together. He stares at the fire as a shadowy figure lurched past a doorway. Fire gleamed from the shoulder epaulettes as the figure crumbles, the gray wool jacket engulfed in flames. The stench of burning flesh fills the air. He dreams of such horror often, reliving the night Atlanta burned, but in his tormented mind he is isolated, cast adrift in a dark world of violence and despair. He has no desire to fight, no interest in Sherman's Special Field Order No. 120. He recalls an officer reciting the order, his voice gleeful and proud for having memorized a document of such brilliant strategic value, repeating Sherman's words as flecks of his deceased skin are pulled from his body by the ravens that have descended on the midnight field of the dead: "...should guerrillas or bushwhackers molest our march, or should the inhabitants burn bridges, obstruct roads, or otherwise manifest hostility, then army commanders should order and enforce a devastation more or less relentless according to the measure of such hostility." A devastation more or less relentless. His wife's pale, dead face supplants the destroyed Confederate city, her slender hands folded across her bosom. He waits for her to open her eyes and speak, and in each dream there is a flicker at her eyelashes before Knight himself awakes. That was when the fire was reignited; the flames catching an evil wind and blossoming into a relentless inferno. His knuckles are bleeding after beating one of his wife's killers to death. His knuckles are always bleeding, and in his ulcered belly a pile of blistering embers that can always be fanned into a raging fire...

The arrowhead had gone deep into the fleshy part of

Reid's shoulder and when Knight yanked it free the skin had torn. Hardly fatal, but nasty enough that Reid would need to keep that wound clean to prevent infection. Reid was sucking in air and puffing his cheeks, hyperventilating.

"Calm down," Knight said.

Reid nodded, his eyes glazed with fear and pain. Dobbs took the silver flask from his coat pocket and said, "This is gonna hurt." He poured the whiskey on the wound and Knight wrapped the shoulder with a long cloth Dobbs had in his own possibles bag for just such an occasion. Knight pulled the bandage tight not caring if it hurt. When he was finished, he picked up the arrow and broke off the bloody arrowhead and handed it to Reid who stared at it with his jaw hanging open.

"Put it in your pocket," Knight said, "and be grateful that you live through this."

Reid lifted his pale features to look at Knight. "Will we live through this?"

"Some of us, I expect. Hard to say."

"Don't you care if you live?"

"I only care about doing my job. If I'm alive at the end of any day then I get another day to do my job."

"Another day of killing?"

"If that's what it takes."

Dobbs, Howell and Sandoval wasted no time in cutting loose the dead horse from the harness. Sandoval was tight-lipped, looking for all the world like a broken man. Darla, being mortified, stayed out of sight in the coach. Knight helped them drag the horse out of the harness and onto the side of the road. It was backbreaking work. They were sweating and Knight cursed fluently under his breath. It took them an hour to unharness the remaining two horses and position them forward. Dobbs wanted to cut the harness down to keep the horses closer to the coach. They cut away the vacant harnesses and Dobbs set to work making certain there were no mistakes.

"Got bushwhacked by Comanches some years back. Did the same thing. Killed two of four and made the ride nearly impossible. Cavalry saved our hind-ends that time. We won't have such a luxury this time."

"It'll be slow," Knight said, "but we'll make the Bear Claw Station."

They all climbed aboard the stagecoach and Dobbs gave an unusually gentle crack of the whip to set the horses in motion. They wanted to get past the scent of death, and as tired as they all were, there was no choice but to move onward. The horses seemed less skittish; their minds involved now in the steady clip-clop of their forward motion.

It was bright and warm and nothing like the storm-tossed forest of an Indian ambush, but the dappled sunlight masked the uncaring nature of a landscape that had recently witnessed murder. They rattled along at an agonizing slow pace and Knight wondered if he would be proven wrong. Making the Bear Claw Station might require a providential hand that he questioned time and again.

The sunlight coming through the trees was deceptively beautiful; almost cool in its texture. There were low-slung clouds tossing occasional shadows and Knight imagined how easy it would be if Vincent Two Hatchets had commanded a larger force of men. They would be annihilated. Not that many years had passed since the 7th had ridden toward the Little Big Horn and discovered the Lakota, Northern Cheyenne and Arapaho possessed an unforgiving memory. Knight understood the cold touch of history and the echoes of Custer's men being slaughtered would never fade.

He thought about Vincent's demeanor as he rode a

horse that he was certain belonged to Cole Tibbs, and he felt cold even though he was sweating from the warm weather. He had seen a man stumbling on the forested hill, and that had to be Tibbs, and he was obviously a prisoner. Whatever outcome this venture suffered would come down to Knight's decisions. He had to begrudgingly admit that Vincent Two Hatchets had out-maneuvered him at every turn. The simplicity of his quest as a lawman assisting Seth Bullock had transformed into a convoluted, bloody skirmish on the trail to Cheyenne.

Dobbs had gone silent, content to hold the reins while chewing a plug of tobacco. They went at a snail's pace, two miles, then four miles. There was no sound from the coach, but then the horses became skittish. Another half mile and they came to a bend in the trail and as they rounded the corner the horses caught the scent of blood. It took Knight a moment to comprehend what he was seeing. Dobbs reined up the horses and they stared at the head on the top of a lance that had been stuck in the ground.

Flies buzzed in the air. The horses snorted, their ears flicking nervously; hooves clopped at the earth. Howell emerged from the coach, and then Reid. Sandoval came out with Darla and Sandoval said, "God almighty! That's Cal Vale!" Sandoval was ashen, trembling. Darla gasped and stepped backward, pivoted on her heels and bent over to vomit in the brush.

Knight was thinking, let them look. Let them see what men do to each other. Take a good look at the cruelties people are capable of inflicting on others.

He climbed off the stage and ran his gaze over the woods, but his instinct told him there was no danger. Not yet. This was a warning, a visual deterrent. He strode forward, took in a breath as he reached the lance, and pulled it out of the ground, tossing it into the weeds. He saw the head roll into a thicket of berries where the wolves or bears would find it. He turned quickly, regulating his breathing and trying to ignore the stench and the flies.

They were all looking at him. Their stares were filled with disgust and horror, as they should be. They were seeing war firsthand, and for most of them this venture was their first time in battle. They were unnerved, petrified with fear.

"Get in the coach. We need to make Bear Claw Station by nightfall."

There was no argument, no questions.

The day's horror gave way to a relentless plodding, an exhausted push to get away but knowing they couldn't get away. The dispiriting scent of death followed them through the sunlight and through a grove of trees where even the birdsongs seemed like a mocking dirge. The stagecoach lurched, rattled and heaved over hills and curved along thin trails until the hills eased away and they entered an oblong grassy valley where they could see the square, timbered frame of the Bear Claw Station in the distance.

As they approached the station Ernie McGruder emerged from the doorway, a deeply sunburned man wearing a sleeveless cotton shirt, his brown trousers held up by suspenders. His long hair was white, his face worn by the wind and sun, his emerald green eyes shining like polished stones. He was carrying a Henry rifle. His lips were pressed together and his face scrunched up like a man that had just bitten into something rotten.

There was no greeting. No friendly salutation. When he spoke his voice was flat and lacking emotion. "You see any bodies on the trail?"

Knight nodded. "Found a wagon that was ambushed. Wolves got at the bodies."

"That would have been the Forsberg family. Had a

dispatch to watch for them. Sorry they didn't make it."
McGruder looked over Howell, Sandoval, Reid and Darla
as the climbed out of the coach. "There's biscuits on the
table and a pot of coffee simmering on the pot-belly.
Outhouse is out back. These horses look done in. Let's get
them situated and then you can tell me what kind of trouble
is following you."

Dobbs, Knight and McGruder got to work getting the
horses into the barn. McGruder had five fresh horses, one
being his own mount, but he made it clear he didn't like the
worn look of the two they would leave behind. When they
were finished Knight told McGruder everything that had
happened and the wiry old mountain man listened without
comment, his eyes as cold as a winter shamrock.

They went inside and Dobbs changed Reid's
bandage. They all ate biscuits and drank coffee. Sandoval
asked if there was a way to get help from the U. S. Cavalry.

McGruder snorted. "You don't put out a forest fire by
pissing on a burning log."

That settled the matter and Knight said they would
leave the following morning before sunrise. Sandoval and
Darla wanted to leave immediately, the violence obviously
whittling down their spirits. Knight reminded Sandoval that
he was a prisoner and he would be shot if he tried any
malarkey. "Between you and those murderous Indians I
ain't got any hope at all," Sandoval retorted meekly before
slinking off into a corner to sit on bench.

Knight said, "Reid, Howell, you two have guns and I
expect you to shoot Sandoval here if he tries to escape. No
charges will be leveled against you."

Sandoval moaned and looked at his boots, shaking
his head. Darla, who was pale and looked to be on the verge
of hysteria, said angrily, "All I wanted was to leave
Deadwood, start over someplace. Now I'm trapped with
108

you bunch of stinking killers."

"You're not staying here if that's what you were thinking," McGruder said.

"No? Maybe if you were in a certain mood you would have come to see me in Deadwood. What's a woman to you after that?"

"I got a woman in Cheyenne that slicks up my cane for me," McGruder said, "I don't need nothing else."

"You're all crude men, no better than animals."

"That's enough," Knight said, "Darla, we'll get you to Cheyenne. You can catch another stage to Laramie and be on your way."

"You're so confident," Darla said sarcastically. "Don't you ever get afraid?"

"I've seen men blown apart by cannonballs. I'm afraid every day, Darla, but I still put my boots on every morning."

McGruder asked, "Can you skin a rabbit?"

Darla looked surprised. "Of course I can skin a rabbit. I was raised in Kaskaskia, Illinois. I fished the muddy Mississippi when I was knee high and learned how to clean 'em and cook 'em. I learned a lot of things back in Illinois."

"I'll bet you did," McGruder said with a sly grin.

"Don't you get any foolish thoughts in your head. I had enough of horny old codgers like you by the time I was twelve. The Jesuit missionaries smelled like cow shit and never took a bath."

"I haven't got any notions about you at all except I need help getting the stew ready. I've got some rabbits I shot yesterday. Marshal, why don't you help me fetch 'em. I've got another thing or two to say."

They went outside and McGruder said, "There's a dispatch rider coming in about a day. Elisha Jameson.

Tough kid. I'll have him send for a cavalry troop to look into Alistair Devine's station. He'll get back in Cheyenne before you do, if you survive. I know about your reputation, so maybe you'll make it."

"I'm saying we'll make it."

"Well, if you're as tough as they say the beer is good at a grogshop called Smithy's. My gal Arlene works the backroom. You might tell her I miss her but I'll see her soon."

"I'll do that."

They went around behind the barn where McGruder had a small garden enclosed with battered old chicken wire. "I had chickens the first year," he said, "but the bears and wolves made that more trouble than it was worth. I hunt for whatever meat I need and I have some potato's growing." Knight saw three freshly killed rabbits strung up on a line near the potato patch. "Sometimes I get deer, and about six months ago a grizzly came down from the hills so I had bear meat that lasted through the winter."

"Indians ever come around?"

"They like to trade for food. I get that fancy canned food, peaches, beans and such, and I ask for firewood in trade. No winter in this part of the country is ever pleasant."

McGruder had a sack of potatoes in the barn and they took the rabbits into the station and Darla set to work cutting out strips of meat. Howell had found a corner to stretch out on the floor and was fast asleep. Reid was reading an old newspaper and Sandoval had fallen asleep as well.

"You got your hands full, marshal."

"That I do."

"I heard about Vincent Two Hatchets from Elisha some time ago. There's a bounty on his head now, but I don't know how much."

The simmering stew filled the cabin with a pleasant aroma. They ate ravenously, barely speaking to each other. McGruder offered Darla his bed and he made a pallet for himself on the floor explaining that most visitors didn't spend the night, but considering their circumstances he understood.

Howell and Reid slept on opposite sides of the room. Both looked uncomfortable sleeping on the floor, but they didn't complain. Knight was restless and knew he wouldn't sleep much. Knight stepped outside and walked around the cabin and barn, a wary eye on the rolling hills. The light was changing as the afternoon faded, and it remined him of an afternoon at Shiloh. It was this type of tranquil light that bathed the peach trees. The light might catch the brass button of a Confederate officer's coat, and then he would lift his rifle and fire.

One thing bothered him. It picked at him like a persistent mosquito. Why had Vincent Two Hatchets let them get here? Was this nothing more than a game of blood-lust incrementally played out to satisfy Vincent's anger?

Dobbs came out of the cabin and smoked a thin cigar while standing near the corral and looking at the trail that had brought them here. Neither man spoke. They watched the horizon for dust from horses, or movement between the trees in the hills.

Dobbs finished smoking and went back inside. Knight lingered, unable to relax. When the purple twilight darkened and made it impossible to see anything in the distance, he went inside and positioned himself left of the door, and stretched out to sleep with his gun in his hand.

The darkness offered no solace. He dozed, random memories flitting back and forth in his mind like moths wavering about a lantern's light. The cabin walls were thick but he concentrated his hearing on the open windows. A nightwind took hold of the trees for a bit, but he heard nothing else. Howell, Reid, Sandoval, Dobbs and McGruder all snored and it was like the camp the Tennessee river years back. All the warriors resting before battle.

He was awake early and he went outside to watch the sunrise. The horizon was yellow, fragile as a harlot's nightgown, and the air was warm and still. Knight could hear birds chirping out in the hills. He went into the barn and all seven horses had their throats slashed. The barn stank of blood and the scent of death had already attracted the flies. His pulse hammered in his head. He opened and closed his fists with such force that his knuckles cracked. He had heard nothing all night. Nothing. Not a clopping hoof or a whinny. They had killed the horses swiftly and methodically, and now they were trapped.

He left the barn and there was Vincent Two Hatchets sitting astride a horse that most certainly belonged to Cole Tibbs, and Knight's heart sank. Their eyes locked and Knight's fingers played at the leather tong on his Colt's hammer.

"No, marshal, don't do that. I have your deputy prisoner. I want you to think about giving up that chest of gold. Think about it all day. I'll return before sunset to take it, or all of you can die." Vincent Two Hatchets swept his gaze across the sky. His gestured widely with the palm of his left hand. "Marshal, it makes no difference to me because I'll have that gold soon enough. it's a good day to die."

Chapter 12

"Give him the gold!" Reid said, a desperate tone in his voice. "There's no way out for us! He'll let us live once he gets the gold!"

"You don't know that," Howell said, "He's on a killing rampage. We have him outnumbered and we need to fight."

"Six armed men against three Indians does give us a better chance," McGruder said as he sipped a steaming cup of coffee. "I'd rather fight. Killing them horses was low, even for an Indian."

"Howell, you can mine more gold!" Reid snapped, "Hell you've got half a million already! That strongbox can last a man a long while but it won't make him a millionaire! Give the Indian his gold!"

McGruder pulled himself out of his chair and looked at the strongbox which they'd shoved beneath the table. "Thing is, just in case I die, I'd like to see the gold we're fighting for. Can't say that I've ever seen a box that big filled with gold."

Knight was watching Howell. His face showed concern. Howell and Knight made eye contact and right then Knight knew that Howell knew there were rocks in the strongbox.

"We can't open it," Howell said.

"Why the hell not?" Reid was panicking. Here it was, Knight thought.

"I left the key in Deadwood. A second key is at the bank in Cheyenne. We can't open the strongbox."

"We didn't discuss that," Reid said, sounding flummoxed. "I put the gold in myself and I locked this strongbox."

Howell looked confused. "As the manager of the Homestake Mining Company it was my responsibility to make certain this strongbox was properly secured. It can't be opened. There's no key."

"It doesn't matter," Reid said, there's plenty of gold

in that box, plenty!"

"Is there?" Howell said. He was looking closely at Reid.

"Of course there is! You just said so. Give the Indian the strongbox and he can shoot the lock off!"

"And he'll find rocks," Howell said, "as you know. What's going on Reid?"

Knight understood it all then in the span of a heartbeat. "He replaced the rocks with gold, Howell. He's complicit with Vincent Two Hatchets."

Reid was licking his lips, his face pale. "You hold on one goddamn minute, marshal! You were supposed to protect us, but look what happened! Those Indians are butchering people, and if giving them the gold saves our lives then do it!"

"The deal was to bait him with a story about gold but we filled the strongbox with rocks. I did it myself." Howell was seething with anger.

Knight said, "McGruder, you have a hammer?"

"Out in the barn. I'll fetch it."

McGruder went out and Knight turned his attention to Reid. He stepped up to Reid with a catlike grace that was at odds with his tough, weathered appearance. Knight's Colt was in his hand. "Let me have your gun, Reid?"

"My gun?" I haven't done anything wrong! Howell was in charge here!"

"You're saying there's gold in that strongbox?"

"Of…of course! I wouldn't say it if it wasn't true!"

"Seth Bullock told me the strongbox was to have rocks, not gold. The gold story was bait to lure Vincent our way so I could bring him to justice. Seth Bullock is a man of his word. If it's gold in that box then I'm arresting you."

McGruder came in with a hammer and Knight said, "open it." McGruder pulled the strongbox from beneath the

114

table, bent his knees and busted loose the lock with a swipe of the hammer. He unlatched the leather buckles and flipped open the creaking lid.

The strongbox was filled with gold bars and leather pouches of gold dust. Howell's face turned red with anger. "By God you filthy fool! You had no right to put our gold in that box!"

"You can't blame me!" Reid squeaked in protest," You got no proof! It could have been Howell just as easily as me! You have nothing to arrest me on, marshal! Nothing!"

"Tell it to the judge when we get to Cheyenne."

"This has been bungled from the start," Howell said, seething with malice. His hate-filled eyes clawed at Knight.

"Don't push me, Howell."

"So what do we do?" McGruder asked, "give up the gold or fight?"

"It's a fight any way you look at it," Knight said, "so we'll give him the gold and see what he does. I expect a fight."

"And the Homestake Mining Company loses a sizable bankroll. Who will reimburse us for that, marshal?"

"Let's survive this first, then we'll figure that out."

"That's the only sensible thing I've heard you say since I got on the stage in Deadwood."

The harsh snap of Howell's tone hung in the air and rather than stand there while everyone shuffled their feet uncomfortably, Knight turned his back on the room and went out for some fresh air. The horizon was clear and the rolling hills seemed ready-made for a picnic, except the persistent buzzing of the flies inside the barn shattered the illusion of tranquility.

McGruder came out with Dobbs and the three of them stood silently in a row staring at the weathered slats of

115

the barn doors a full minute before McGruder said, "Can't tolerate this. Those horses didn't deserve that. Never heard of a goddamn Indian mistreating horses like this. I can't stand it."

Dobbs, chewing a plug of tobacco, said "Lot of work to bury 'em."

"No, take too long. I've been thinking I'm going on to Cheyenne now. No sense keeping the station open, especially if old Alistair Devine up at Mule Creek Station made it to the bone orchard. No, I'm thinking about burning the barn. That'll send a clear signal to Elisha, the dispatch rider, that something's wrong. He's our best hope for reinforcements."

Dobbs nodded, spat a brown glob at the ground. "I'll help ya."

They took lanterns and shook the oil onto the hay and at the timbered walls. The stench in the barn was nauseating and they worked quickly. Dobbs and Knight stepped aside and watched McGruder strike a wood matchstick to his trousers and the small flame licked at the stale air. Then McGruder tossed the matchstick into the hay. Knight knew it had to be rough, but McGruder didn't complain.

The barn burned swiftly. The others came out of the cabin and stood near the corral as the flames curled into crackling dragons and chewed at the boards. After some time they could smell the burning flesh of the horses and Darla covered her mouth with her hand and sobbed.

Knight approached Darla and said with an uncharacteristically soft tone of voice, "Darla, go on inside."

McGruder eyed her appraisingly as she walked into the station cabin. "Looking forward to getting into Cheyenne once this is done. Haven't seen Arlene in many months."

"We've got some work ahead of us before that happens," Knight said.

"You've got a way about you, marshal, that isn't always pleasant."

"I don't wear a marshal's star to make friends."

"I can see that."

"I want the trunk of gold brought here," Knight said, gesturing at the corral gate, "I'll ask for the hostages to be released. Then we'll see what they do."

"Seems odd for him to take the gold, leave any hostages and then ride on." Dobbs was scrutinizing the distance ridgeline. The brush and pines faded into the distance. "Vincent Two Hatchets is outnumbered but that doesn't make me feel any safer."

"Let's say he takes the gold and rides on," Howell said, "what then?"

"That dispatch rider can bring help. We need horses. If we don't get horses we walk to Cheyenne."

"It's been done," McGruder said, "but it will take a few days and leave us open to being massacred."

"If somebody has a better idea," Knight said, "let me know."

"It's only three goddamn Indians!" Howell said. "We have six armed men! They can't do anything to us!"

Reid, looking forlorn and dejected, said, "This has all gone wrong!" He put his hand on his wounded shoulder and grimaced.

Knight was thinking that all men are plagued by insecurity, greed and lust and here were four of six men who might die because their minds were clouded by the vagaries of their circumstances. Of Dobbs he had no reservations. The old stagecoach man would fight well. The others were crippled by fear. Knight understood that, too. Sandoval and Darla had it the worse. The fear had eviscerated them. The West did that to people. Out here in the high country the brutal landscape caressed your senses, cajoled you and teased you with its vision of Eden, and then took it away with the swift and merciless strike of a serpent.

In his travels, Knight had seen at least three small settlements the pilgrims had named Paradise, and each place had been ripe with malice. It was always the same. One man's vision of Paradise was inevitably at odds with another man's idea, and Paradise became just another hell hole on a trail leading to Boot Hill.

But it hadn't always been that way. Even after the war he had somehow managed to cling to this idea of Manifest Destiny and the Promised Land. He took a wife and he ached for her still, decades after her death. They had settled in Cherrywood Crossing and Knight became a farmer. The Colorado Territory was wilder then, untamed, and how he wished he taken her east into the Ohio River Valley. The outlaws had come to Cherrywood Crossing because of their greed, their desire for wealth, and after robbing the bank they had spurred their mounts, galloping hard to escape and giving no thought to the woman who was trampled under the hooves of their panicked steeds. The day's brightness was dashed into shadows that seemed like another world that revealed itself as the destroyer of peace. It was like having a dark demon that crouched in his soul and fed from his grief, keeping itself alive by living off the anguish of his tortured mind. One day, he thought, that beast would devour him...

They watched the barn burn and crumble, a slithering line of black smoke crawling skyward as the crackling timbers settled into a smoldering heap of dark ashes. Knight ordered Sandoval to stay inside with Darla. The rest of them would take up strategic positions around the cabin, distancing themselves so as not to be caught in a crossfire.

All afternoon the tension clung to them as they waited, fidgeting; all except Knight who remained as immobile as a statue, whatever demons that nipped at him held in check by his strong will.

In the mid-afternoon the wind picked up and the shadows came alive with each gust; a flurry of scampering silhouettes as the trees cast a regiment of unfriendly shades when the leaves fluttered and the branches bent against the pressure of epileptic breezes.

Reid looked forlorn, his face drawn, the whites of his knuckles showing as he clenched and unclenched his hands. Dobbs was calm, the only sign of stress in the veteran infantryman was that of his right boot tapping out a rhythm to a drumbeat only he could hear. Howell boiled with anger and Knight half expected the mining executive to explode with violence, his gaze sometimes tossing daggers in Knight's direction. McGruder appeared saddened, the loss of the horses marking the end of his career as a stage line station manager. Knight went into the station once to check on Darla and Sandoval and found them so desolate and unhappy looking that he promptly turned on his heel and resumed his position near the corral.

If this was God's plan then God was a malicious potentate who took pleasure in the misfortune of his creations. Knight lifted his chin and looked at the fragile blue sky; a flawless heaven that seemed like an endless banner of brightness over the hillsides of white spruce and tall juniper trees that made a green canopy on the southwestern trail to Cheyenne. He studied that trail but there was no dust, no sign of the dispatch rider. He took a deep breath feeling the uncertainty pressing on his shoulders, an invisible weight that exhausted him.

The silence settled around them, and the sky drifted ever so slowly into twilight. Through the trees Knight could see the blue transform into a pale yellow and the spaces between the trees grew darker. He heard a horse whinny followed by the clop of a hoof. The air had cooled, and the sweat dried on him. He felt alert, ready, the lassitude suddenly vanishing.

Looking east, and down the hard-packed road that had brought them here, Knight saw the outlines of two men, a horse between them as they walked. He recognized the silhouette of Cole Tibbs. They were leading a packhorse. There was no one else on the road. When they came closer Knight was relieved to see that Tibbs looked to be in good shape, maybe a little haggard, but otherwise unscathed. Lucky. The other man was a stranger to him, but that had to be Breen.

"Cole, sorry you ran into trouble."

"Yup. They have rifles on us. We're to pack the gold in these canvas sacks and take it to Vincent Two Hatchets."

"I'll help you pack it up," Knight said.

"To hell you will, mister! You saw what they did to Cal? We're gonna do what we was told! We ain't doin' nothin' but bring him the gold."

"You must be Breen."

"They killed all of us. I'm trying to stay alive!"

"Sandoval is inside."

"He can stay there! It's his fault this all happened!"

Knight ignored him, concentrating instead on his friend. "Cole, how do want to play this? We're six strong with guns against three Indians."

Tibbs waved his hands urgently. "No, no, Max, you don't understand, there are…"

Knight saw the flaming arrow in his peripheral vision, and before Tibbs could finish his sentence the arrow slammed into Breen's belly. Breen opened his mouth and wailed, a high tortured scream as he fell to his knees, his hands clamped onto the arrow, the flames licking at his fingers. The immediate response from behind Knight was gunfire from Howell and McGruder, but they were shooting at shadows.

Breen fell to his side, blood on his lips. His shirt and hands were smoldering. The dying man had managed to pat the fire out but there was no chance he'd survive. The arrow was almost halfway into the bowl of his belly. Tibbs sprang toward Knight, throwing himself to the ground. For a moment Knight was disoriented and he crouched low, craning his neck for a look over his shoulder. He saw Dobbs looking around desperately for an Indian to shoot. Reid had his back to the cabin wall, gun in hand, but he wasn't firing. McGruder called out, "Where the hell are they?" The pack horse had bolted up the road and as Knight turned his head he saw several figures emerge from the darkness and a sickening realization took hold of him.

"Tibbs! Are you hurt?"

"No, but it's no use! No use at all!"

Knight watched the Indians take the horse's reins, and he counted five, and two more horses. His mouth was dry, like a man that had woken up after a night of too much whiskey. He yelled out, "Stop shooting!"

Off on his left, at the cleft of a hill, he saw four shadowy figures. Tibbs crawled over to him and Knight gave him his Winchester. "We'll fight, Cole. We won't quit."

"There's…"

"More than three. Yeah, I got that."

As the sky darkened the Indians lit torches, and holding them aloft, they formed a line on a distant hill. Some minutes later another group of three lit torches and appeared in the distance, this time west of Bear Claw Station. Knight counted twelve flickering torches. They were surrounded. The Indians had drawn the battles lines and there was nowhere for the group trapped in the cabin to go. In the eerie silence they all came forward and watched the shadowy figures holding the torches. Knight snapped, "Darla, get back inside!" A few times over the course of the next hour two or three at a time would call out in their native language; shrill calls that echoed ominously down to the beleaguered group. There were no other challenges.

Dobbs eased himself over to Knight and Tibbs. "I've seen this before. They aim to scare us, make us lose sleep. They'll attack in the morning. This fella Vincent Two Hatchets is clever and careful like a fox."

"Hell," Knight rasped, "I don't even know which one to shoot first."

"He's waging a war," Tibbs said, his voice laced with fatigue.

"Looks like he's winning," Knight said, and then he told everyone to get inside. McGruder threw the bolt across the door and shuttered the windows. The shutters had rifle slots and Knight looked out at the torches as another flurry of Indian yowling echoed from the dark trail.

"Listen to them growl at us like animals!" Howell grunted. "Savages! It's like nothing I've ever seen or heard before!"

"They got the gold, don't they?" Reid said, his voice small and whiney.

"It's still out there with Breen," Sandoval said, "I think Breen is dead by now."

"Think long and hard about that," Knight said.

"What the hell does that mean, marshal?"

Knight ignored him. "Cole, what can you tell me?"

"The old man at Mule Creek Station is dead. Vincent Two Hatchets has an informer in Deadwood. He knew I was following."

Knight cocked an elbow and pointed his thumb at the others huddled around the table. "That would be Reid over here."

"I'm surprised you haven't shot him."

"Might soon."

"Who's the woman?"

"Darla, a whore."

Tibbs nodded. "Those Indian boys won't waste a second riding her after we're all dead."

"She's got a derringer in her purse." Knight looked at Darla. "Darla, shoot yourself with that purse pistol when the time comes."

"You disgusting men!" Darla spat the words venomously. "We're all gonna die and you men are too stupid to save us! You hear me? You're all nothing but pigs!"

"None of us are dead yet, Darla, except maybe Sandoval here." Knight glanced at Sandoval. "With you, I reckon dying is just a formality."

Sandoval turned white and retreated to a corner where he sat down with his back to the wall, a broken and pathetic man. After that none of them seemed talkative and they settled down, taking turns looking through the shutter rifle slots, but there was nothing more to see. The flaming torches had been removed all they saw was the pure, chilling darkness of a wilderness night. Some of them eventually fell asleep, Reid first, and then Howell. Darla was restless and Knight was grateful when he noticed that she too had fallen asleep. Dobbs, McGruder and Knight took turns keeping watch. Knight didn't care much if he slept or not. The darkness and uncertainty add to all their miseries, and for Knight what had seemed like a simple plan to trap a stagecoach robber had descended into a hellish and ignominious tactical failure.

He didn't feel bad for any of them except Cole Tibbs. The young deputy had a fine woman waiting for him, just as Knight had once had a fine woman. Now they were facing certain doom. He had some sympathy for Darla. He didn't like her at all, but what small measure of sympathy he could muster from the dark recess of his bitter soul he might reserve for her. The rest of them had played the game and understood full well the unwritten code of life in the high country under Western stars. Take it and don't complain. Work at it like a man should. Face the consequences like a man should.

The long night stretched into a hazy pale horizon and when McGruder said it was time they opened the door and stepped out into the first glimmerings of a calm morning in the Wyoming Territory where the dispatch rider, Elisha Jameson, sat astride his horse watching them, his face beaded with perspiration and his shirt bloody. The burned barn was still smoldering on the boy's right, and Knight noticed the gold was gone. Breen was cold and dead and ravens pecked at his flesh.

The boy said, "I got word back to Cheyenne. Saw the smoke and knew it was trouble. Stopped at the old hermit's shack."

"Come down from that horse,' McGruder demanded, "I'll tend to your wounds."

"Couple of arrows hit me is all," Elisha said, slipping out of his saddle. Knight was impressed by the boy's constitution. "That old hermit hates the Indians and says he'll ride to Cheyenne. He might have made it."

"Remi Fournier," McGruder said, "I trapped beaver and hunted elk with him some years back. Didn't know he was still around."

Elisha looked at the ruins of the barn. "Horses?"

"Gone." McGruder's voice was hard. "We've got our

hands full here."

"Yup, that you do. I've got a Winchester and extra cartridges in my saddle bag."

McGruder took Elisha into the cabin and Knight walked with Dobbs around the corral to study the hills. If Vincent Two Hatchets and his men were nearby they were well hidden. There was no sign of them; no dust trails, no scent of campfire smoke. They had blended into the landscape like ghosts.

But in the valley and across the rows of sagebrush and into the pools of light growing amongst the pines, the morning was coming alive, and with it would come the sound of guns. The fight was inevitable. Vincent Two Hatchets had made certain they were trapped. Knight didn't think they would have to wait long at all.

Chapter 13

When the rooster crowed Knight saw a plume of dust in the east and then another dust trail rising in the west. Vincent Two Hatchets had sent his men galloping in opposite directions, circling Bear Claw Station, yapping and hollering. Knight instructed everyone to stay inside and wait. Once the dust hung heavy in the air the Indians unleashed a volley of rifle fire. The cabin was riddled with bullets, forcing everyone to keep low.

Dobbs, watching with a critical eye, remarked, "If I can get a bead on any of them I'll send them along the hallelujah trail!" Before Knight could protest, Dobbs slipped out and ran crouching toward the smoking ruins of the barn.

McGruder, fuming with anger, barked, "I'll take my chances outside! Those bastards bleed like the rest of us!"

The Indians set a dangerous, rampaging pace as they

circled the cabin, and Knight begrudgingly admitted his admiration for their horsemanship. Most of them rode bareback, skillfully utilizing the bridle and reins, their heels biting at the horses, urging them on. He could smell the rancid odor of the dead horses as he skirted around the barn, the embers still steaming a day later. Most Indians revere horses, tend to them carefully, but Vincent Two Hatchets had overseen the callous slaughter of the stage line horses, only to have his men demonstrate their equestrian mastery as they taunted him with their yapping and shrill calls.

He noticed that none of them paused to take aim; they were firing randomly, seemingly intent on creating chaos. He winged a shot from his Colt at the blurred sight of a galloping brave, knowing that he missed, and feeling foolish for the effort. He heard Dobbs trigger his shotgun somewhere behind him, followed by a guttural curse. Another round of gunfire closer to the cabin indicated that McGruder was attempting to take the fight to the Indians, and Knight hoped a lucky shot or two found its mark.

The Indians were wasting ammunition, which meant they had plenty, while McGruder and Knight were gambling. The odds were against them. He heard Dobbs cussing again and then firing. So far, no Indians had been hit. Gunsmoke and dust from the horses shrouded the sunlight that was igniting the landscape as the morning brightened.

Knight was crouched ten feet from a stinking, smoldering heap of burnt timber, squinting at the wild Indians racing past, their figures swathed in dust while above them a sky broke free of the mist, blue as a bird's egg. The sunlight warmed the air and made the dust feel like hot ash on his lungs. The whirling curtain of dust was like a warm blanket, thick and stifling. He heard more gunfire, and lost in the heat, the echoing voices of Howell and Reid screaming insults as they tried to shoot an Indian off his horse. It was a useless endeavor.

Knight hauled himself to his feet and began running, trying to intersect one of the galloping Indians as they came around on his right. A shot plunked into the ground near his boot just as he narrowly avoided being trampled by a brave's horse. He had a glimpse of the Indians as he twirled sideways, his knees bent. He was shocked by how young the Indian looked. The horse whinnied, bolting away.

A clattering sound caught his attention. When he craned his neck and peered over at the cabin, he saw McGruder climbing onto the roof. He mounted a barrel, struggling to pull himself over the eaves. There was a flurry of rifle fire and a blanket of dust briefly obscured his view. He thought he saw McGruder tumble, and when the dust cleared the old station man was nowhere to be seen.

Howell was cursing up a storm. Horses thundered past him and Knight had a glimpse of him with his teeth gritted, his gun in his hand belching hot lead as he fought bravely near the cabin doorway. Then Nick Sandoval pushed his way past Howell, his face etched with desperation. He had a Winchester in his hands and he began firing, levering a fresh round into the breech, firing and levering over and over until the hammer clanked onto an empty breech. Howell screamed, "Get inside you damn fool and reload!" But it was too late. Two fast shots from a Henry repeater and an Indian yelped with victory, a high bold shout. Sandoval screamed, too, but his was a keening acknowledgment of his death as the bullets tore his chest apart, blowing through him; gouts of blood pooling around him as he fell, his eyes fixed on the empty, lonesome heavens.

For a long moment Knight was convinced they were doomed, but then Howell shouted, "Got one!" as an Indian

127

jerked spasmodically as he fell from his horse. The circling band of Indians began to disperse, cutting loose from the swerving, noisy attack. Scattered gunfire followed the retreating Indians, but Knight understood that this was no victory. This was simply the beginning.

When the dust settled he warily approached the cabin where Howell was standing over Sandoval. "Dumb bastard died like a fool."

"You got one at least," Knight said as he walked over to the fallen Indian, a boy of no more than sixteen. "Good shooting," Knight said, but his words fell flat. There was no sense in this, no sense at all.

Knight and Howell found McGruder's body along the cabin's side. A bullet had punched a neat red hole in his left temple and then shattered his skull when it exited at his right temple. They lined up the dead Indian and Sandoval next to McGruder, leaving them in a patch of sagebrush forty feet from the corral.

Elisha Jameson was sitting at the table with Darla who surprised them by appearing calm. She had wiped the tears off her face and looked composed. She looked up at Knight and Howell. "Well, you're not dead yet, are you!"

"Just checking on you, Darla. You look better."

Darla raised an eyebrow. "Oh, really, marshal? Men don't usually care about me except when I'm on my knees with my mouth full."

"There's no call for that kind of talk!" Howell said.

Darla laughed. "Look at this one here," she said, pointing to Elisha. "We had a good time because we thought we might die."

Elisha was blushing furiously. Knight ran his palm thoughtfully over his unshaven chin. He was surprised, but then again, he thought, *hell, why not*, although he wouldn't say it. He did say, "Look kid, keep your trousers buttoned.

We need you helping out with a gun in your hand."

Darla made a sour face. "You have something against having fun, marshal?"

"McGruder is dead out there. He was a good man."

"I'm sorry, marshal, I really am!" Elisha sounded truly repentant. "She got to fiddling with her bodice and I don't know what came over me!"

Howell snorted derisively. "This is the dandiest thing I've ever seen! Darla, you ain't nothing but a worthless whore! Playing with a boy when good men are fighting on your behalf! We ought to leave you for the Indians!"

"I might be better off with them!" Darla said with a sneer.

Howell stepped forward and raised his hand to strike her, but Knight stepped in his way.

"No, you won't do that."

"What the hell is this? You have a soft spot for this whore?"

"Her and the boy are victims of circumstance. The rest of us knew what we signed on for. They had some fun so leave it alone. It's over."

"Didn't take long either," Darla said grinning, "We thought we might be killed, and besides, I like 'em young and clean like him."

"That's enough." Knight was thinking that Darla knew how to set things in motion. It must be second nature to her. "Elisha, take your rifle and stay outside on the porch. You two can get married once we get to Cheyenne."

Elisha went out still red in the face. Darla gave a throaty laugh. "Married, my ass! I gave that boy something nice to remember. What the hell does a mangy lawman like you know about marriage anyway?"

"Not a thing, Darla, not a thing." He should have let it go, but as he turned away a flame flickered to life and

129

heated him up the same way a long glass of whiskey warms a man's insides. He turned around and faced her. "My wife was killed by outlaws. I know what I'm missing, but I know mostly the good things she never got to have. That sticks with me. She wanted a child. So I don't blame you and the boy at all. It's like you said, you thought you might die. I'm glad you didn't. I'll try and keep it that way."

She gave a little cry, like something was caught in her throat, and he saw the tears in her eyes. Turning his back on her, he was aware that Howell was following him outside. Howell grabbed Knight by the elbow to slow his stride. Knight resisted the urge to hit him again. He'd done that once already, but this wasn't the time to do it a second time.

"Marshal, I want you to know I'm going to write a letter to the U. S. Marshal's office, maybe even to my connections in Washington. I'm going to document how you bungled the safekeeping of the gold that belongs to the Homestake Mining Company."

Knight was only half listening. As Howell was chewing him out he realized one of their group was missing, and he had a fair hunch where he'd gone to.

"That's fine, Howell, just fine. Now why don't we all look around to see where your friend Reid has disappeared to?"

Knight organized Tibbs, Elisha, Dobbs and Howell to look around, keeping close to the perimeter of a hilly plain that bordered the station. It took them less than fifteen minutes to determine that Herbert Reid of the Deadwood Bank had vanished.

"He's gone to find Vincent Two Hatchets," Tibbs said.

"He set us up!" Howell snapped, "I should have shot him!"

Dobbs, chewing on a wad of tobacco, said reflectively, "How long can a man live who bargains with the devil?"

Tibbs was pacing restlessly; he seemed tired and silently angry. Knight decided against approaching him. He wondered how rough it had been when he'd been held prisoner in Vincent Two Hatchet's camp. Tibbs was a good lawman, one of the best that Knight had seen in the service. Their job was unenviable, often deadly, but no way to get rich. A marshal's job didn't offer a salary that helped a young man who was thinking about starting a family. He knew it was closing close to the time when he expected Tibbs to cut himself loose from the U. S. Marshal's service. He could do better in a wide variety of other occupations. Tibbs was smart and people liked him.

The Indians attacked suddenly, a high-pitched warrior's yell piercing the tense silence. Three of them came galloping near on horseback and shouting challenges in broken English. "Come white fools! Come die with us!" Their horses seemed possessed by a demonic speed as they flashed past the eastern side of the corral, another gout of dust rising from their clopping hooves. The dust made a veil across the eastern range.

"Yip! Yip! Yip!" echoed with the cadence of furious steeds stomping at the earth, yet the Indians never fired their rifles. Another group of riders repeated these actions on the western side of Bear Claw Station. Howell fired at the fleeing figures, but his shot accomplished nothing. Knight yelled out to stop shooting and Elisha and Dobbs lowered their guns.

A shroud of doom hung over them. They were helpless, and all of them seemed to realize it at once. The Indians contented themselves with shouting challenges and circling them to keep the dust swirling. The beleaguered group didn't have enough ammunition for a prolonged battle, and Knight expected the station cabin to be burned. That, by itself, was a risky tactical move on the part of Vincent Two Hatchets. The smoke, like that of the barn when it burned, might alert the ranchers outside of Cheyenne that there was trouble. It was a gamble, but if Elisha's story about the old mountain man bore fruit, help might come. The sight of smoke would confirm that Bear Claw Station was under siege.

Just as these thoughts flashed through his mind, Knight saw the first flaming arrow arc through the dust, sizzling with animosity as it sped downward and slammed into the cabin roof. It was followed by two more arrows. Knight told Elisha to fetch Darla before the whole place burned down around her. He brought her out, her lips tight but much calmer than she had been. Maybe she was resigned to her fate.

Knight was acutely aware that they had limited cover. With the station cabin burning, the best they could do was crouch low near the blackened remains of the barn. They've got us, Knight thought. He wasn't thinking about himself so much as he was the others. He harbored a vague hope of catching a glimpse of Vincent Two Hatchets so he could shoot him.

There was a slow cessation of horses galloping in circles. It took them a few moments to register the fact that the Indians had retreated. None of this made any tactical sense to Knight. Vincent Two Hatchets was obviously a man intent on doing things his way.

Bear Claw Station burned.

The smoke was thick and black as it spiraled like a living thing into the sky. It was like a twister operating on the solitary point of a log cabin, and the flames crackled almost gleefully. He turned to speak to Tibbs but it was

Howell who was standing near him.

"He went off," Howell said dully.

"Tibbs? Where?"

"How the hell would I know where! He went is all, west, running low along the brush line. The fool might make it."

Knight was surprised. Tibbs was no coward. Running wasn't like him, but he had run. Knight felt hopeful rather than disappointed. Tibbs deserved to live. He had a future. This was a rotten deal.

"Cheyenne is a long way," Howell added. "Maybe someone will see the smoke."

Darla walked past them to the well pump, jacked the squeaky handle until the water spluttered out. Taking the ladle she filled it and drank it all down in one gulp. She wiped her mouth on the sleeve of her now filthy dress. She licked her cracked and dry lips.

"Nice cool water. Don't you cowboys sing songs about cool water? It's a lifesaver except when every goddamn Indian is trying to kill you."

"A woman has no call to speak in that manner," said Howell.

Darla turned her head slowly and observed him with the same level of disgust she would use in looking at a scorpion. "What are you supposed to be, Mister Howell? A right proper gentleman? You dally with Diane at Swearingen's Gem. A right proper establishment. Word is she's the only one who can make your manhood rise because your wife can't. Isn't that right Mister Howell?"

"That's enough out of you!"

Darla leveled her gaze at Howell and Knight felt her anger like a hot wind buffeting them. "I hope I live long enough to watch all of you die first! I hope the Indians make you suffer!" She spat the words, then turned on her heels and went to stand near Dobbs and watch the cabin burn.

To come this far and fail. Knight felt small in this enormous landscape of imposing mountains. The wind picked up and destroyed the black smoke as the cabin was eaten by the flames, the ashes speckling the blue sky like fragments of decay on a dead man's face. Grief is the price of caring but Maxfield Knight had toughened himself against such aspects that weakened a man's character, but there it was, covering him like a raw, red sunburn that offered no relief. He wouldn't bend. He wouldn't give them the satisfaction.

Of course it wasn't to be. He would remember it years later, too, standing here beneath a cloud of acrid smoke with three people that didn't much care for him, and Dobbs, a fine old wrangler. He could only hope that Tibbs made it.

The finality of the last timber turning black and settling into the ash with a crumbling moan left them all feeling hollow. He could see it in their faces. Darla stood off to the side with Elisha, Howell fifteen feet away, isolated, angry. Dobbs was smoking. His insatiable appetite for tobacco seemed to revitalize him. The old man rarely showed signs of fatigue.

They waited. There was no reason to start walking toward Cheyenne; no reason to make an effort at hiding. They all knew it, so they waited. Then after some time there was a stirring of dust and the Indians began appearing. Their appearance was quite sudden and skillfully accomplished. Four Indians appeared on the northern perimeter, one on a pinto which Knight knew the Sioux favored. Most of the others had mustangs. They were surrounded and then Vincent Two Hatchets appeared, still mounted in the saddle of Tibbs' quarter horse.

Vincent Two Hatchets had stopped far on Knight's right, and facing the west. Knight heard Howell mutter, "Why don't they get it over with?"

Vincent Two Hatchets spurred his horse and it moved five feet and by then Knight had his gun up, but Vincent Two Hatchets stopped and held up his palm. He called across to Knight: "This fight is over. Keep your guns but put them away." Knight looked around at Howell, Dobbs and Elisha. They were nervous but none of them opened fire.

"What do you want?" Knight drawled.

"Come to our camp. We have food and water. I wish to speak to you, marshal."

"What if we don't?"

"Then you'll die."

Knight holstered his Colt and looked at Dobbs who shrugged. They all stared at Vincent Two Hatchets who never flinched. Howell said, "I don't trust him."

When Vincent Two Hatchets spoke next, his voice was strong and loud, and none of them would ever forget the monarchial dignity his voice had when he lifted his chin and said, "Marshal, are we not blessed when thy king is the son of nobles, and thy princes eat in due season, for strength, and not for drunkenness?"

None of them answered, mostly out of shock, and there was a lengthy stretch where all they heard was the movement of the horses; a swishing tail, the clop of a hoof. It was Darla who broke the silence, stepping forward and announcing, "Well I'm hungry, you goddamn fools! Let's go!"

So it was that for the first time in his life U. S. Marshal Maxfield Knight voluntarily surrendered and went to have a meal in the camp of his enemy.

Chapter 14

Herbert Reid was in the camp and Knight had to restrain Howell to prevent him from killing the Deadwood banker. He was standing near the fire nonchalantly smoking a cigar and Howell got in one good punch that bloodied Reid's lips and sent him reeling backwards. Vincent Two Hatchets observed this with a bemused expression.

Suddenly Knight was surrounded by the Indians. They pulled him away and in the same instant relieved him of his gun. He heard Howell protest as his gun was taken. The kid Elisha and Dobbs were also disarmed.

"You said we could keep our guns!"

"We have a matter to settle first, marshal."

"What matter is that?"

Vincent Two Hatchets nodded at several young braves who promptly knocked Reid to the ground, rolled him onto his belly and tied his hands behind his back. Reid was stunned and started to blubber in fear. "What is this? We had a deal! What are you doing?"

They tied his ankles and Reid wet himself. He knows what's coming, Knight thought. They all knew it. Darla turned away but the rest of them watched. They lashed a rope up high around an oak branch and lifted him, his head swinging just inches from the ground.

"I wasn't supposed to get hurt," Reid said, and he sounded like a petulant child. You've got the gold! I wasn't supposed to get hurt at all!"

"This man has betrayed you," Vincent Two Hatchets said as he stepped forward. "His lies are the same as any white man I have known." He pointed to the strongbox of gold resting off to the side. "He betrayed you for gold. Was it worth it? You set a trap for me, marshal, but Reid switched out the rocks. I was asked to kill you all so that

Reid could have half of this gold. With the other half I will barter for guns and cartridges to wage my war."

"Then why bring us here?" Knight asked, "Why not kill us back at the station?"

"My mind has changed because you have a woman with you, and because I respect you marshal."

Darla turned to look at Vincent Two Hatchets just as he took his tomahawk and cut open Reid's belly with two hard swipes that burst him open, his bloody intestines dangling before his eyes. Reid screamed and then Darla screamed.

Even as Reid hung upside-down looking at his own bloody guts, the young Indian boys, most no more than fifteen, had prepared gutted and skinned rodents, rabbits and squirrels over the fire, letting them rotate on spears of whittled maple branches. The air was filling with the scent of cooking meat which mingled with the stench of Reid's eviscerated intestines.

Elisha turned abruptly aside, lurching into the brush to vomit. Darla was gagging and coughing. Knight went to her side and gently lifted her by her right elbow, steering her away. His stomach clenched, his mouth shut, but by God, no, he wouldn't bend.

The Indian boys were efficient in cooking the meat. Small animals, especially those freshly killed like these, gave off a pungent aroma, and Knight found himself remembering a Confederate camp where they had captured, tortured and Killed a Union officer, afterwards propping up his disemboweled corpse against a tree while they feasted on grouse and pheasant.

Knight's stomach growled involuntarily.

"Oh God!" Darla was rasping. "God help us! Oh please God!"

The meat was sizzling on the spit-roast, the faint

smell of maple lingering with the smoky squirrel and rabbit meat when Reid's innards expunged a blackened gout of shit and blood as his body went into a seizure and his eyes turned to the color of dull glass.

"You must be hungry, marshal," Vincent Two Hatchets said as he took a darkened piece of rabbit leg and began chewing. The Indian boys and some older Indian men took turns eating. Elisha and Darla retreated to the camp's perimeter; Howell and Dobbs across the camp. There was no chance of escape. Knight could see that Vincent Two Hatchets had a disciplined albeit small force of men with him.

Knight watched the Indians eat, and they ate everything, not wasting one chunk of meat. They even ate the smaller bones, grinding them with their teeth. Knight sat on a fallen tree trunk and ate some small fragments of rabbit. The sun had gone behind the tree line when Vincent Two Hatchets added small branches to the fire. His eyes reflected the licking flames and Knight felt as if he were looking into the eyes of the devil.

"You look at me as if I am something unholy." Vincent said without looking up. "But I am not the cause of this."

"We all control our destinies in part," Knight said. "What makes you an exception? You brought this on yourself!"

"Did I? If the dead could speak my wife would tell you a different tale."

"Your wife has nothing to do with this."

"Oh yes she does, and so does yours. I know about you. The famous marshal who never quits. You ride a long trail under a lonesome sky, and death follows you."

"You're educated, but you speak lies."

"I was educated by the white man. I speak your

language as well as a teacher. The white man refused to help my wife and she died, and white men killed your wife. Tell me, marshal, did you allow the white men that killed your wife to live? I heard a story once. They say you beat a man with your fists. He died slowly. If this is true, then we are like brothers because the man who refused to help my wife also died slowly."

"We are nothing alike."

"I am going to tell you a story. For the white man, the sky is empty and without meaning. For the men of my tribe the sky is alive with the spirits of our fathers. This is where I see my wife, and the great Lakota warriors. My wife was a good woman. She went to the boarding school as did I, and she learned the white man's way. She had Jesus in her life as the white man wanted, and she did not complain. She was to give me a child, and then she was ill. I took her to the white man's doctor but he said she's a heathen, and he wouldn't help her."

The flames crackled around the branches. "I told the doctor she was white too, that she was both, and he said he knew that. He said she was a half breed and her blood wasn't pure. That's how a white Christian man thinks. I told him I also had white blood, but it didn't matter."

The fire crackled and the Indians began to drift out of sight in a circular manner. They obviously had planned to watch their prisoners, but it was guesswork where in the darkness the sentries were posted.

"His name was Doctor Samuel Cornwell, and he died as Herbert Reid died today. A man that died looking at his own guts."

"I would have arrested him, brought him to justice."

"A white man's justice is soft like a feather."

"He would have hung. Because of him two station keepers died. He was an accomplice to murder."

139

Vincent Two Hatchets was silent then, his eyes fixed on the flames as night closed in around them. Knight was sick of listening to him. Dobbs and Howell had settled down to sleep next to a tree; Elisha was sleeping on the ground but at a respectful distance from Darla. He was about to slide off the log and sleep. They wouldn't kill them that night, and he wanted to be ready for whatever was planned for daybreak. He was drifting off when Vincent Two Hatchets spoke again.

"A man reaches a point in his life when the nightmares start. It's confusing. Why now? What have I done to cause these nightmares? They tire me out. Why can't I live in peace? Men like us will never live in peace. Can't you see that, marshal? You and I will die violent deaths."

"But I can fight to the end. Won't you give me that chance?"

Vincent Two Hatchets shook his head. "I am releasing you tomorrow. I want you to deliver a message."

"What message?"

"I will get to that. I have something to speak of. You know of this, what fear does to a man. I feared losing Aiyana, my wife. I could not think of living without her. Now my sleep is filled with fear. Where does this come from? I avenged her death yet I cannot find peace."

Knight didn't know what to say.

"You are troubled by my talk?"

"I can't think of any way to help you except to arrest you and let them hang you."

"At the school, the younger ones sometimes died. Many girls who had been raped by the white men. Their bodies are hidden. There is a field of graves near the school where the yellow flowers grow in the summer. I think each flower is the soul of a murdered child. I want you to tell

140

your government that. Tell them the ghost children are singing songs of freedom. They have risen into the sky and they are free. The white men cannot escape these children."

Vincent Two Hatchets stood up and walked away, leaving Knight alone near the fire.

They had been on the farm a year when she started talking about having a child. When the chores were finished he sometimes sat with her out in the pasture and they talked about the names of boys and girls, and what names they might choose for their child. In the late afternoon, his favorite time of day, the sun brightened the shadows as it began to sink into the west, and she always remarked at how beautiful the trees were. He said he would make a swing from a rope and a wood plank so their child might play here, and they could make a picnic on a blanket. Then he remembered the look in her dead eyes, the brightness gone...

Reid's cold eyes caught the last of the dwindling fire, his body a silent shadow towering near him. A night breeze nudged Reid's body and his intestines squirmed like bloody snakes set loose upon the world. The marshal turned away, but he couldn't sleep. He stood up, careful not to wake the others, but aware that he was being watched. None of the Indians were visible, but he could feel their presence. A moment after he stood up a young brave stepped into the fading firelight. He was holding a Spencer rifle and looked at Knight impassively. There was a sound behind him so they had had two sentries awake and watching.

He thought about what Vincent Two Hatchets said about letting him go, and he had to believe he'd let Darla go as well. He would ask for that. He would ask Vincent to let them all go if he hadn't already planned to do so.

Elisha was stirring. The boy sat up looking at Knight. He saw the Indian guard and rose slowly to his feet. He nodded at the marshal and stepped carefully toward him. They spoke in hushed tones.

"You should sleep, kid, save your strength."

"I know. Look, marshal, I wanted to explain."

"No need. I understand."

Knight couldn't be certain in the dim light, but he thought Elisha was blushing.

"It was my first time. She's pretty."

"I understand."

"Don't you think she's pretty? I never expected this to happen."

"You're a man and a man needs a woman now and again."

"I'm going with her, all the way to San Francisco."

"Did she say that?"

"She said as long as I love her when she's old, we'll have a good time."

"You'll meet other nice women. Isn't Cheyenne full of them?"

"Darla's been dreaming about getting away. I've never been anywhere but here."

"I see."

"Don't you have a woman now, marshal? I mean I heard about your wife. They say you hunted down her killers. Is that right?"

"You ask a lot of questions."

"I heard that Indian say he was releasing you."

"I'll be asking him to release all of us. Get some sleep."

Elisha settled down and the night closed in once Knight sat down with his back to a tree trunk to sleep. The Indian guards blended into the darkness. They certainly didn't like it when he was on his feet and moving around. He dozed. He pushed away the night sounds and the sounds of life that plagued him, and he prayed he wouldn't dream about the dead. Let their voices be still this night while I prepare myself for Vincent Two Hatchets.

When the dawn broke, a golden sliver at the world's edge, he heard a raven calling and his mood plummeted. He was the first one on his feet and he turned his gaze westward. Vincent Two Hatchets came out of the trees followed by his small army of twelve warriors. There was dust in the air, and Knight realized a company of horses had caused that dust. They were coming toward them, men on horses, and Knight knew what that meant. Apparently, so did Vincent Two Hatchets who observed the dust cloud with a calm demeanor.

"You're friend Cole Tibbs made it three miles west and should be joining with the men from Cheyenne soon." He said. "We shall fight today."

Chapter 15

Vincent Two Hatchets broke camp and herded them out of a deep section of the forest and closer to the Cheyenne trail. Mounting their horses, they made certain they were seen, inviting the riders to approach under the white flag of truce. One of the Indian boys had taken the bandanna from around Reid's neck, whose corpse was left hanging upside down in the clearing, the bloodstains clearly visible on the bandanna.

An hour later they learned that the old mountain man that Elisha had spoken with, Remi Fournier, had gone to Cheyenne and reported an uprising. The sheriff, Tobias Millson, had organized a group of ten hard-scrabble cowpunchers to see what was happening and put an end to any trouble. They were all members of the Cattleman's Association and in no mood for Indian trouble. Cole Tibbs, as Vincent Two Hatchets had stated, had met them on the road.

Tibbs had reported the murder of Alistair Devine and Ernie McGruder while telling the sheriff about the stagecoach. Sheriff Tobias Millson himself had ridden up close to the Indian camp and called out for a parley. Sheriff Millson demanded the release of the marshal and the other stagecoach passengers. They had fifteen minutes to release them and then they would attack. Knight admired the man's grit.

"We will enjoy killing these men," Vincent Two Hatchets said happily. He seemed delighted by the prospect of battle. "We are evenly matched. The men who die will have a good death."

Knight was astonished by his confidence. "You can't be certain you'll win? Those are tough men. They see you as a threat to all of the territory."

"As well they should, marshal."

Sheriff Millson cantered back to the group where Knight caught a view of Tibbs looking even worse than before, but at least he was alive. Tibbs looked pale and near exhaustion.

There was one deviation from the sheriff's demand that none of them were prepared for, although later Knight would admit they should have seen it coming. Rather than wait fifteen minutes for the Sheriff and his men to understand that Vincent Two Hatchets had no intention of surrendering, the Indians immediately attacked.

In a clever ruse, four Indians came galloping in from the north, their horses chomping hard at the bit as they tore loose another wave of dust. Knight had no choice but to marvel at their skill which was matched by their enthusiasm. He had never seen such a willful enjoyment of battle. Such was their skill that several arrows cut the air with a lethal whooshing sound, and sheriff Millson was the first man hit. He took an arrow in the meaty part of his left leg, howling in pain as he tried to rein his horse around in retreat.

Knight saw Tibbs lift his rifle and begin firing. Knight was helpless without a gun and he yelled for Darla and Elisha to stay down. Howell and Dobbs had disappeared, no doubt running for cover.

Three additional riders came at the sheriff's posse from the southwest, taking them by surprise. These Indians were using rifles and they killed one man instantly. Knight saw the man topple from his saddle, his rifle flung from his grip as he fell. Knight wanted that rifle so he waited until the Indians circled out of view, the posse now in full, panicked retreat. Scrabbling low but moving fast, Knight found the rifle and checked the breech. The poor man hadn't even fired a shot.

He heard the "Yip! Yip! Yip!" cries of the Indians followed by a thundering echo of gunfire. Men screamed in the distance, either from being hit or from fear. A glimpse of the faces of the young warriors whooping with joy as they fearlessly attacked a group of hardened cowboys who were learning a hard lesson about Indians had Knight thinking they had lost.

The damn heart of it all was that he understood the madness. He felt it inside of him, like the cold touch of a serpent's skin, a lashing out with as much strength as he could muster. To kill, to tear them apart, to make them suffer, all those and those like them that had taken her from him, and may God have mercy on his soul for he would never stop hunting them…

Boots stomped the earth behind him and Knight spun around to see Tibbs running toward him. "Jesus! Max, stay down!"

"I need a horse!"

Then Darla screamed. They heard her wailing north of them, not far from where Vincent and the sheriff had parleyed. Knight started moving in that direction when Tibbs grabbed his arm.

"We can't go that way! They'll cut us down!"

They went west, slipping into a dry arroyo before coming out into a hilly switchback which they followed into the hills. The sounds of the gunfight receded, but occasionally they could hear the Indians taunting and yelling at the sheriff's men.

They climbed silently and when they reached a hilltop they looked back and saw several bodies strewn across the valley – two Indians and two cowboys. Nothing decisive had happened. Knight wanted to take the fight to Vincent Two Hatchets, but Tibbs protested.

"Look around, Max! They have too much cover in these trees and the hillsides are steep! They know this land. They were born here. We're strangers and they have the advantage."

Something in the tone of his voice made Knight pause. Tibbs was right, of course, but there was something else. The deputy was tired. He'd been pushed to his limit.

There was another ridgeline near them, thick with pine, and they could hear the Indians still taunting the posse. It wasn't like those men to scatter in fear and Knight hoped they were re-grouping to come at the Indians with guns spitting lead. A direct, fast assault seemed like the best approach. Neither Tibbs nor Knight could determine the exact location where the posse was located, but they decided their efforts should concentrate on joining them. So far Vincent Two Hatchets had succeeded in surprising and scattering the posse, forcing them to retreat after killing two of their men. Sheriff Millson wasn't having a good day.

146

The second wave of the battle began when they heard shooting on the opposite ridgeline and they saw Vincent Two Hatchets on his horse as he emerged from a copse of white pines. Even seen at a distance, Vincent Two Hatchets was a figure of power; strong and proud except for the glittering shadows that pulled at his eyes. Maybe it was a trick of the sun and shadows, or maybe Tibbs and Knight had lost their grip and succumbed to fear, although they would never admit this. Either way, Vincent Two Hatchets was a towering image of death. The shadows of the trees playing across his features made him look bestial, grinning like a Death's Head, his long hair looking cobwebbed and catching the light as if it were burning.

In order to join the fight, Knight and Tibbs would need to climb down the hillside and cross a treacherous rocky valley before climbing again through a forested hillside. They hadn't realized how effectively they'd all been scattered across a treacherous terrain. The distance was less than a mile and they expected to encounter some of the Lakota warriors, but they started downhill all the same.

When they reached the bottom they were visible to anyone perched on the hillside above them, so they weren't surprised when a rifle shot shattered against a rock formation so close to Knight that fragments of rock and dust were dashed into his eyes. He cursed, wiping his face with his hand.

Looking up, Tibbs said, "I don't see the shooter."

Another shot smashing into the dirt in front of them sent them back, halfway into the tree line. They couldn't cross that narrow valley while a rifleman had them in his sights. They decided to veer left through a hanging woods where the branches dipped low over the animal trail, obscuring them from view. They began ascending the ridge until they saw the shooter.

"He can't be more than twelve years old," Tibbs said dismally.

"He's trying to kill us," Knight reminded him.

Tibbs was silent as they began stalking the Indian. They briefly lost sight of the Indian and because Knight was anxious to rejoin the fight, he stepped out of the brush, and then quickly stepped back just as a shot rang out and the Indian boy exposed himself by stepping into the sunlight himself. The risky bait had worked and Knight shot him and he dropped like a stone. They pressed on, passing the corpse where Knight checked the body to make certain he was dead. Tibbs wouldn't look at the corpse and passed by quickly, his face drawn.

It had taken them forty minutes to circle around after Vincent Two Hatchets had initiated the attack, and once they crossed the Cheyenne trail again they saw two Indians torturing one of the cowboys. They had knocked him from his horse, disarmed him, and were dancing around him with obvious joy as they swiped at him with bone-handled knives. Their knives were red with blood and the cowboy's shirt was slashed apart, soaked with crimson.

The cowboy was brave, tough, cursing at them and doing his best to strike at them with his fists. But he was tired, an overweight man unaccustomed to such constant battering. They wore him down. Knight slammed his rifle to his shoulder and was about to fire as one of the Indians leapt at the cowboy, his knife glinting wickedly as it easily sliced through the cowboy's neck, his jugular vein spouting blood.

The two Indians saw Knight and Tibbs. Knight fired but they had deftly sprinted into the brush, nimbly zig-zagging with the ease of deer avoiding a predator. The cowboy was dead when they reached him.

Knight was looking for Darla and Elisha but there

was too much dust and everyone had apparently separated, taking shelter in the forest. That didn't stop Vincent Two Hatchet's men from hunting them down. Knight and Tibbs took up positions on the southern side of the Cheyenne trail, about thirty feet from each other, and began to fire on any Indians that came into view. They soon realized their effort was useless. When they heard a man screaming they ran toward the sound of his voice and found another cowboy butchered near the smoldering remains of the station barn.

Dobbs was nearby, chawing on some tobacco and reloading his shotgun. "Went back for it," he explained. "No sense in letting these Indian boys get away with everything."

"Where are the others?" Knight asked.

"Can't say for certain. Darla and Elisha ran off together. She was screaming her head off. Haven't seen Howell. I expect they must all be dead by now."

Knight noticed that Dobbs was bleeding on his left arm. "You're hit."

"War arrow. Rubbed some tobacco juice onto it since my whiskey is all gone."

"We'll clean it and bandage it when we get a chance," Knight offered.

"Let's find Vincent Two Hatchets," Tibbs said irritably, "I want my horse back."

Finding the Indian renegade would turn out to be a challenge that none of them would forget. A furious gunfight between the Indians and the sheriff's posse had taken lives on both sides, but in the end the sheriff and his men were skillfully herded off the trail, over a ridge and into a box canyon. It was a stalemate.

Sheriff Millson and his men were hunkered down inside the canyon with good position on the rocky high ground halfway up a switchback. There was nothing the

Indians could do to hurt them, but at the same time the cowboys had no leverage over the Indians. To make matters worse, Vincent Two Hatchets showed no inclination to leave.

Knight, Tibbs and Dobbs found shelter half a mile away where they discussed their options, none of which were good. As Knight and Tibbs watched the canyon it was apparent that Sheriff Millson had no intention of sitting tight. His sharpshooters were poised in the rocks while three men moved up the switchback. They were looking for a way to get higher and come back around for a better angle to fire down upon the Indians. The men moving up the switchback wouldn't be visible to the Indians on the ground. Once again, Knight had to admire the sheriff's grit along with his good sense. Having never met the sheriff before, he hadn't known what to expect, but from what he'd seen so far he wasn't the type to run and hide.

Knight and Tibbs remained hidden near a long clump of creosote brush and an hour later there was a flurry of activity in the canyon. To their astonishment, the sheriff and a few men came galloping out of the canyon and screaming curses like warriors of ancient times. They whooped and hollered, firing their guns at the Indians who promptly retreated. Knight had never seen anything like it. Although he was wounded, the sheriff's attitude and demeanor was anything but defeated. He had rallied his men and were taking the fight to Vincent Two Hatchets whom Knight was convinced had to be as surprised by this turn of events as he was.

The West was like this, Knight knew; there is no shortage of wild tales of Indian fights where brave men engaged in the horrifying business of killing. There were brave men on both sides, but only one group would live to tell these lonely, brutal stories of survival. It was still too early to determine who might survive the fight, but sheriff Millson and his men had taken it upon themselves to make it a good fight.

A young Indian's head exploded from a .44 bullet, the breeze dispersing the blood and brain matter like a misty, red rain. Sheriff Millson and his men were on horseback and Knight understood they had a better chance on horseback than on foot. By managing to keep their horses in the first bloody moments after their arrival had given them a tactical advantage.

Vincent Two Hatchets himself had vanished, and Knight was fearful that he would get away. Then he spotted him galloping toward a small eastern mesa where the trail surrounding it offered a protective wall of pine and ash trees. Several Indians followed him. Knight decided to go after them, albeit on foot which was foolish, but Tibbs followed him without question as he knew he would.

There was no hope of overtaking the fleeing killers, but Knight wanted to be nearby when the sheriff and his men converged on Vincent and his men. When the sheriff and four men came galloping onto the trail they were ambushed by three Lakota warriors. Jumping from behind the cover of small pinon trees, their bullets slapped into the sheriff's horse which let loose an agonizing wail as its legs buckled, blood gushing from the wounds with the same ease as water from a hand-pump. The sheriff cursed as his horse fell sideways and nearly crushed him as they struck the ground.

Just as quickly as they had appeared, the Indians disappeared. Knight and Tibbs ran to the sheriff and pulled him out from beneath the dying horse. The bandage on his injured leg was red with fresh blood, but he was otherwise unhurt.

Sheriff Millson, grunting in pain as he was pulled

from under the horse, cast a cold look at Knight and said, "Thanks, marshal, these boys are giving us a good fight today."

The sheriff's men were sitting astride their horses looking on. Knight said, "Let's take the fight to them. You've managed to get them running."

The sheriff continued to impress Knight. He wasn't a tall man, although the dime writers would later exaggerate his height; he possessed that same hard stare that gave men reason to pause when dealing with marshal Knight.

Gunfire popped over the ridge and Tibbs said he thought Vincent Two Hatchets was backtracking to Bear Claw Station. The forest and hills surrounding the station would offer cover and that's where they expected a showdown. Getting there, however would be a problem.

Flushing with excitement, and encouraged by their momentary success, sheriff Millson and his men gathered some horses and went off the main trail. Millson wasn't going to let being shot off his horse stop him from saddling up again. They started cantering toward the gunfire with Knight, Tibbs and Dobbs following on foot. It wasn't an ideal brigade, at least not by Knight's estimation, but Vincent Two Hatchets had managed to prolong this encounter much longer than even he had wished for. They all moved warily, pushing through the scrub oak and gnarled greenery as silently as possible.

One of Millson's men, who had been separated from them when the shooting started, staggered into view. He was bleeding from being nicked by some arrows, but was otherwise unhurt. He was embarrassed, frustrated and exhausted, none of which made any difference to the sheriff. "Follow along as best you can," Millson barked, "and try not to get killed." Knight thought, at least his presence had added a gun to their group. Millson wondered out loud if the remainder of his men had been killed.

The pulled themselves sluggishly over a hill of thin, white pines and a sound made Knight spin around, but the path behind him was empty. Still, he had a feeling they were being stalked and he said so to Millson. The grizzled sheriff reined his horse and gazed down at Knight, his attention taking in Tibbs and Dobbs as well.

"You've managed to stay alive a long time, marshal, so I'll trust your hunch. We all need to spread out. Clumped up together like this would be like shooting ducks in a pond."

They drifted apart, moving methodically northwest where Bear Claw Station had to be a hundred yards ahead of them. The arduous trek back to the burned husk of the station wasn't something that bothered Knight. He had been in greater peril, and Millson's tenacity added a much-needed level of strength. He was beginning to think that Vincent Two Hatchets should be considering a major retreat, but he also knew such a retreat wasn't possible. Vincent Two Hatchets would fight until the end.

They were wasting time. In the span of several hours they had fled the burned station, veered after the posse into a canyon, engaged in a haphazard gunfight, and circled back to the area surrounding Bear Claw Station. A glance at the sun's position told Knight the afternoon was upon them. Vincent Two Hatchets and his men had the advantage of being able to traverse the terrain with greater skill than any of their pursuers. They were encouraged only by their ability to force the Indians to flee.

They encountered Howell, badly wounded, hiding in a thicket of berries which Tibbs reminded him was foolish because the area was populated by bears. When they pulled him out of the brush he had an arrow in his side and a bullet wound on his leg. The bullet wound was superficial but the

153

arrow wound was serious. The arrow had entered his left side and exited out the back. It didn't appear that any vital organs had been hit but he had bled too much. Knight thought he had less than a fifty-fifty chance of survival. It would all come down to how he handled the infection that was certain to come.

Tibbs and Knight took control of cleaning Howell's wounds themselves. Knight cut the arrowhead off the shaft and examined it. Sometimes Indians coated the arrowhead with the poisonous juices of various plants or even animal dung, the intention being to infect their enemies so that they died by fever if the arrow itself didn't kill them. Knight knew this was often an effective tactic and difficult for some people to recover from. He didn't see any visual evidence that the arrowhead in Howell had been contaminated in such a manner, but there was no way of knowing for sure. They would only know by how well or how poorly he might become in another day or so. If he was going to die, it would be fairly quick, but unpleasant.

Knight asked that they build a fire so that he might sterilize his Bowie knife. It was a risky move to stop and build a fire when there was a pause in the pursuit, but Knight told them Howell was in a bad way. If they didn't cauterize these wounds, especially the stomach wound, then he might die. He was pleased and impressed that sheriff Millson agreed to work toward stabilizing Howell. Enough good men had died. As for Howell himself, he was conscious most of the time and seemed noncommittal, almost as if he were resigned to dying. Knight snapped at him once, telling him, "You better not die after all this work Tibbs and I are doing to save your carcass!" At this, Howell could only meekly shake his head in gratitude, his body already warm with a coming fever, and rasp: "I'll live long enough to write a letter of complaint about you, marshal."

154

With a tight clump of gathered branches, they had a fire going. Soon the Bowie knife was steaming hot from resting in the flames, and Knight cauterized the entrance and exit wound, the acrid stench of burning skin nearly forcing Tibbs to turn away and vomit. Knight didn't hesitate to cauterize the bullet wound as well.

Howell, who watched all of this with a baleful stare, never flinched. Knight made certain the belly wound was sealed, pressing the knife hard against the skin which sizzled and smoked, but the bleeding had stopped. Knight had been through it all before, and he had seen men scream in agony when the hot blades were pressed against their flesh. In a way, it was like branding a man. The scars would stay with him forever.

Dobbs helped bandage Howell, wrapping his chest as if he were a mummy, and it was then that the mining executive muttered his thanks through clenched teeth.

"I'm beholden to you, all of you."

"You can pay for some chewin' tobacco and a tall glass of beer when we get to Cheyenne," Dobbs chided.

"My life is worth the price of tobacco and beer," Howell lamented, but his sour mood had dissipated. He even gave Knight a half a smile when the marshal helped him to his feet. Tibbs kicked dirt into the fire and quickly stomped it out. He reminded Knight and the others that every moment wasted could prove helpful to Vincent Two Hatchets.

Tibbs called out a warning and pointed up the winding trail. They all turned in unison and saw that he was pointing at Vincent Two Hatchets and four warriors, all on horseback, and plummeting in their direction, an acrid plume of dust animated by their steeds writhing skyward. No sooner had this scene registered on their minds than the shrill cries of the angry Indians pierced their consciousness with the same sharp and lethal effect of a cannon burst.

They must have felt the time was right for a counteroffensive and once again Knight thought that he had underestimated the circumstances. Tibbs told Howell to get into the brush and keep down. Dobbs ran across the road and used the trees for cover as he aimed his shotgun at the marauding Indians. Sheriff Millson and his men scattered on horseback, their rifles ready, but it was already too late.

There was no time to shout orders; no time to prepare for an onslaught from five galloping men intent on killing all of them. No time at all. A bullet crashed into a deputy's eye, exploding from the back of his skull, his blood and brains splattering against the gleaming tin star on Millson's vest. The dead man's horse shrieked, the scent of blood driving the horse into a frenzy. The body toppled from the saddle and the horse reared high on its hind legs, spun and crashed its iron-shod hooves against the dead man adding further indignity to his death.

Dobbs' shotgun boomed but the blast caught only air as he was forced to dive deep for cover as a wicked volley of gunfire tore up his position. Tibbs sent several shots at Vincent Two Hatchets whose fierce countenance would be forever etched in his memory. Knight shouted commands uselessly, his voice lost in a cacophony of gunfire, yipping Indians, neighing horses and galloping hooves. Knight saw the sheriff retreating into the forest, his horse jumping fearfully over the brush.

The madness continued as another deputy took a bullet in his shoulder, and then another bullet tore apart is chin. He screamed as he fell and an Indian galloped toward him. With swift finality, the Indian shot the downed deputy and raised his rifle and gave a victorious whoop. Knight aimed for the Indian but missed yet again as the brave heeled his mount and bounded out of sight. Tibbs was looking desperately for Vincent Two Hatchets.

Dobbs had reloaded his shotgun and let loose with both barrels as a brave galloped into view. The force of both barrels discharging knocked the crouching Dobbs onto his ass, but the blast struck the Indian in his chest and he flew backwards from the horse. Dobbs was after him, reloading quickly; shaking loose the two spent shotgun shells and slipping two fresh rounds into the barrel. Then with a calm and efficient movement, he lowered the barrel to the wounded Indians head and pulled the trigger.

Sheriff Millson had dismounted, leaving his horse out of view in the brush. He came loping toward Knight, fuming with anger. "Are you goddamn blind? Can't you shoot straight? We need to kill these fuckers!"

A bullet tore into Millson's bicep and he reeled back, grunting. Knight stood straight and tall, unscathed, and Millson and the others watching would remember the moment the rest of their lives. Millson stumbled backward, jumping in the brush for cover while Knight slowly turned on his heels, arm outstretched, his Colt unwavering in his hand. He thumbed the hammer and pulled the trigger. His bullet struck an Indian at the precise spot where his heart would be and another Indian galloping toward him reined his horse to a halt and screeched. Knight shot him as well, his Colt booming with an ominous echo.

Tibbs came and stood next to Knight, his rifle barking as he picked his targets carefully. The Indians circled and once again Knight, Tibbs and the surviving posse were driven back by an onslaught of rifle fire.

Dying under such circumstances was bloody and lonely. Knight and Tibbs found themselves continuously pressing forward, but to do so they were forced in and out of the surrounding woodland's cover. Once they dashed through a clump of wheatgrass and found a dead deputy. He had been struck by two bullets in the chest and had crawled here unseen to bleed out. His face, frozen in the rictus of death, was a picture of anguish.

The air was reverberating with the hissing sound of bullets, the moans of the dying, and the guttural, protesting neighing of horses pushed to their limit. Sheriff Millson was staggering through the sage and taking cover behind an ancient oak tree. They had rallied twice, been beaten back, and now only the few that remained alive, on both sides, were engaging in a last effort to claim victory.

Tibbs was thirty-five feet on his left when they both were attacked. Knight felt a presence moving in the brush near him and then an Indian came vaulting free of the greenery, leaping effortlessly at him with a bone-handled knife that arced dangerously close to Knight's throat as the Indian slammed into him. They both tangled up, falling to the ground. Knight's gun swung around, his thumb clicking the hammer into position, but when he fired the Indian had twisted deftly aside and the roaring blast of the gun caught the Indian on his right ear, creasing his skin. The Indian howled but Knight doubted he could hear himself from the gun discharging so close to his ear.

The blade cut the air, swishing back and forth near Knight's head. Knight had been pushed onto one knee, the Indian clinging to his shirt, and it took him longer than it should have to push the Indian aside, and then cock and fire his gun again. He sat there catching his breath as the Indian slumped to the ground and quickly died.

Tibbs had been stalked by Chaska who managed to knock the rifle from the deputy's hands. The ensuing fight, with both men using only their hands, played out almost silently. Knight, watching from a distance, felt surreal as the two men pummeled each other, pushed, tripped and slammed each other around with the only major sounds being the impact of their bodies or the flat sound of a fist striking flesh. Knight could tell that both men were breathing heavily. Tibbs had his teeth clenched, perspiration dripping down his face.

Without a weapon, the fight would come down to skill and strength, and maybe a little luck. Knight checked his Colt and thought about aiming for the Indian, but he couldn't be certain that Tibbs wouldn't be hit. He tried to push himself to his feet but that's when he felt his age, and he sucked in air trying to get his strength back.

Chaska was getting the better of Tibbs. He knew it, too, and Tibbs did something that he rarely did. He prayed. It wasn't much of a prayer as far as that goes, but it was something, and it was a simple prayer asking that he might live to see his woman Jamie again.

Knight eventually managed to get moving, got up close to the two grappling men, and rather than risk a shot that might injure Tibbs, he brought his arm back and bludgeoned the Indian with the Colt. The impact tore a crimson swath across the Indian's skull, knocking him senseless.

Tibbs could barely speak. His mouth was dry and black dots swam before his eyes. The two exhausted lawman gaped at each other over Chaska's unconscious form.

"Took you long enough," Tibbs rasped.

It was an odd moment of comradery amidst the chaos. The fight, however, was far from over. Knight saw the remnants of Millson's posse converge at the trail; Howell was limping along after them. There were but two deputies left alive, although they wouldn't learn that until later when the found the bodies. Millson, his last two deputies, Dobbs, Howell, Tibbs, and Knight went relentlessly looking for Vincent Two Hatchets. They wanted to fight with no one else. They were of one mind, and Knight recognized this although he remained silent. He would bring Vincent Two Hatchets to justice, and if he captured him alive he would watch him hang.

A feeling of ecstasy had overcome Knight, and he welcomed it. He had felt this way before, and if he remained a lawman he knew he would feel this way again. It was a fever of confidence; a blood-lust only men in battle understood. It gave him strength.

He had felt it the first time at Shiloh with the scent of blood and horses and eviscerated men dying in the tall grass as the cherry blossoms scented the breeze. And that nugget of fear that rested in his soul was part of it as well; a heavy weight that reminded him that he was mortal and all men shall pass from this earth and into the Lord's hands, but first there had to be battle, and such battles are moments of pure, abject terror. It writhed in his belly like a snake...

With an echoing roar of hatred, the Indians came at them again. Blood stained the trail and the wind carried the snapping punch of a gun, the screams of men, the frightened whinnies of horses. The remaining deputies died; their horses died. There was no mercy this day for men or their horses. The thump of a tomahawk against a man's bone, the shrill guttural intake of a man's final breath, his body convulsing as he bled out.

Vincent Two Hatchets rode like a demon, his features carved into a face of vengeance, and Knight saw him and shouted out to him: "Come and fight me, you fool! Fight me like a man!"

But Vincent Two Hatchets was not so easily swayed, and he thundered past Knight on his horse without a second glance. Infuriated Knight screamed, "You let your wife die! You left her alone to go seek a white man's knowledge!

You failed her, Vincent, just like I failed my wife! Now let us fight like men!"

At this, Vincent Two Hatchets reined his horse, turned, and came at Knight again. The tomahawk was in his hand, the blade shiny with blood as he thundered down on Knight whose gun barked again, and he thought he hit him but then he was knocked aside, the tomahawk slicing air.

"You honor your wife's memory by killing innocent people," Knight bellowed, "There's no honor in that, no honor at all!"

Once more his horse was reined hard, turned fast and came at Knight like a tornado. Vincent Two Hatchets had a tomahawk in each hand and he leaped from his horse, arms flailing, and Knight felt a blade strike his arm as the two men crashed into each other. They hit the ground hard enough to knock the breath from both of them,

It was Tibbs that saved him. He came over to Vincent Two Hatchets and slammed the butt of his rifle against his head. Blood welled from the wound, and Vincent Two Hatchets slumped sideways.

Knight groggily stood up as Howell came limping toward them, a gun in his hand. "Don't let that heathen scum live! Shoot him now or I'll shoot him!"

Tibbs and Dobbs stepped in front of Vincent Two Hatchets and Tibbs took the gun out of Howell's shaky hand.

"Why didn't you kill him?"

"My gun was empty, but now he can stand trial." Tibbs said.

Howell was fuming but said nothing further.

With Vincent Two Hatchets and Chaska taken prisoner, Tibbs turned his attention to Wapasha. He was astride a palomino not forty feet away, a rifle in his hand. Tibbs scrutinized him carefully and told them he thought

Wapasha was about to fight even though he expected to die. It was a matter of honor for the young brave. Sheriff Millson, however, had other ideas.

"I'm going to hang all three of these dirty killers right here. We're not waiting for a trial and we are not putting them in jail and feeding them. I'm going to hang them, marshal, and I'd like to know now if you'll try and stop me."

Millson had his hand on his holstered gun. Howell, in a physical acknowledgment of agreement, had also turned to face Knight, his gun ready. Knight had it figured that he could rely on Dobbs and Tibbs, but he didn't like the set-up. Going against another lawman was a rotten deal, and he said so.

"What good will it do to take them to Cheyenne? You know the judge will immediately sentence them to be hanged. These men are killers. I knew both Alistair Devine and Ernie McGruder a long time. These men butchered them. You may not like it, marshal, but the law accommodates an officer when he's under duress while riding with a posse. There's not a judge in all this territory that would find fault with hanging them."

"While you two are arguing over killing him, It looks like Wapasha has made up his mind." Tibbs said, gesturing toward the Indian.

Tibbs was right. Wapasha raised his rifle over his head, pumping his arm and shouting a war whoop. His heels dug into the palomino's flanks and it bolted into a gallop. Wapasha could be heard yelling, "Yip! Yip! Yip!" as he dropped his reins and aimed his rifle at them. The first shot went high but that didn't matter. Tibbs, Dobbs and Howell jumped sideways from the trail, all three firing at Wapasha simultaneously.

Most of their bullets hit Wapasha in the chest but he

remained on his horse. His face transformed from war-like defiance to resignation. He looked at them through a glaze of pain. His horse had stopped, perhaps understanding his rider was injured. The palomino snorted, shook its head, the mane brushing against Wapasha as he slumped forward, hooves stomping at the earth nervously.

Wapasha tried to lever his rifle again for another shot, but Millson shot him with his Colt, the bullet smacking into his throat, destroying his Adam's apple, a gout of blood catching the sun as Wapasha tilted and fell off the horse.

"That only leaves two to hang," sheriff Millson said.

Battles are fought in the heat of madness and unrelenting anger, but are rarely successful because of tactical brilliance. At least that's how it was for U. S. Marshal Maxfield Knight who believed that only the strong survived, but they sometimes needed luck. No matter if luck played a role this day, or if a providential hand was at play, which he doubted, he was grateful that Vincent Two Hatchets had been stopped.

Sheriff Millson locked wrist irons around both Indians, dragged them to their feet and announced he would hang them then and there. Both Chaska and Vincent Two Hatchets never flinched, never showed any fear. Knight thought Vincent Two Hatchets had to be enormously disappointed to find himself a prisoner of the Cheyenne sheriff, but his features never changed. There was no hint of defeat, no regret; only a deep coldness in his eyes, an emotionless glacier that withstood whatever emotions must surely be surging in his soul.

It was Cole Tibbs who reminded them they needed to find Darla and Elisha. None of Millson's deputies had survived, and they suspected one of two Indian braves had survived and fled upon seeing that Vincent Two Hatchets had been captured.

They scoured the area but then logically returned to the burned remains of Bear Claw Station where the fight had begun. Darla was next to the corral fencepost kneeling next to Elisha's body. She was weeping.

Vincent Two Hatchets spoke for the first time in several hours. He was impassive, his voice flat. "The boy died as a man does fighting. His spirit is free."

"You'll be free in a minute," sheriff Millson said. "You're gonna hang."

Darla looked up at Vincent Two Hatchets. She rose slowly to her feet. Her lips trembled when she spoke. All of them were surprised by the sincere emotion behind her words.

"You filthy man! You killed him! He was a sweet boy, and you killed him. It makes no sense! You killed him!"

Vincent Two Hatchets lifted his chin and observed Darla with curiosity. "My wife was a gentle soul as well, and she might have been saved."

"No, no, no! You killed this boy for no reason! He had done nothing to you!"

Knight saw her hand come away from her side, and he remembered too late he had let her keep the little silver purse gun. Later, he would wonder why he hadn't moved. There might have been a chance to stop her, but he didn't move. Darla shot Vincent Two Hatchets between the eyes, the dull echo of the gunshot drifting slowly away.

Knight took a deep breath and said, "Damn you, Darla."

Chapter 16

They hung Chaska quickly but it was a brutal affair. Killing men is not always easy, and hanging a man is especially cruel. Knight had seen it all before. Sheriff Millson had a rope strung around Chaska's neck, looped the rope over a sturdy oak branch, and Millson found a horse and pulled himself into the saddle. He slowly cantered the horse away from the tree lifting Chaska slowly from the ground. He took twenty-five minutes to die, slowly strangling to death. When it was over his face was a deep purple color, his tongue stuck from between his bloody lips. Chaska had voided his bowels when he died and emptied his bladder.

Millson untied the rope from the saddle's pommel, slipped to the ground and tied the rope off at the base of a tree. "I'm going to hang both bodies from this tree," Millson declared. "I want other Indians to see this."

Millson took it upon himself to hang Vincent Two Hatchets' body, tying the ropes off and letting the bodies dangle. By the time had completed his task the flies and gnats had begun swarming around the corpses.

They buried Elisha and the deputies, although they didn't find all of the Indian bodies. Some of the wounded braves must have run off in fear and died in the forest. Millson didn't say it, but the loss of his deputies wouldn't go down well in Cheyenne, but he had witnesses to confirm that everything possible had been done to bring Vincent Two Hatchets and his men to justice.

They found the body of Remi Fournier. Dobbs pointed out the old mountain man had put up a vicious fight before he died. The dead Indian next to him had been pulverized, Fournier's broken rifle next to him. He must have used it as a club right up to the end.

They gathered enough horses for the ride to Cheyenne, and by mid-afternoon the sullen and unhappy survivors started down the trail. They passed the bodies of Chaska and Vincent Two Hatchets swaying from the trees silhouetted against a yellow sky, and Knight thought nothing good ever came of murder. Darla spat at Vincent Two Hatchet's feet as she passed.

All of the gold had been recovered and they packed it into saddlebags under Howell's watchful eye. They were sullen and silent, looking more like defeated soldiers than victorious survivors of an Indian rampage.

Their arrival in Cheyenne was unheralded although sheriff Millson would soon have his hands full with the city council and families of the slain deputies. Knight would avoid that, submit his witness statement through the resident judge, and then leave Cheyenne. Whatever sympathy the sheriff might elicit from the town council would come from them seeing the nature of his wounds.

The sheriff had fought the best battle possible, and even the most jaded and self-serving politician would have trouble finding fault in his efforts.

The solitude of a hotel room gave Knight time to gather his thoughts. He washed himself with the water pitcher on the bureau, but declined to use the hot bath the hotel advertised downstairs. His own scrapes, bloody nicks and bruises were nothing compared to the others. He wasn't unscathed, but he was lucky enough to walk away with minor ailments.

He wrote out a report for sheriff Millson, outlining the facts and being certain to mention the sheriff's dogged determination to halt the Indian attack. The loss of ten men wouldn't be something they'd forget for a long time. Knight suspected that Millson was finished as sheriff in Cheyenne, but his reputation would grow from this. That would be either good or bad. Knight understood that for himself. He felt sympathy for the sheriff.

When he report was finished he smoked as he sat at the window and looked down on the street. Cheyenne was growing since he'd first come through here years ago. The West was changing, sometimes for the better, and sometimes in ways that left a scar across the souls of those brave men and women who ventured across the Mississippi.

Yet it wasn't over. Knight had some loose ends of his own to tie up, and the first order of business was to speak with Howell. They had all checked into the Continental Hotel, courtesy of the town council as an expression of gratitude for assisting sheriff Millson.

Knight waited until after they all had time to wash the dust and blood off themselves to knock at Howell's door. He wasn't pleased to see him.

"Marshal, come in. I suppose you're here to talk me out of complaining about you to the marshal's office."

Howell was thin and pale. It would take time for a full recovery, but Knight thought the man was damn lucky to be alive. He sat in a leather chair looking across at Knight. He was weak, but trying his best to appear strong and able.

"No. Complain as your conscience dictates."

Howell was surprised. "Then what is it? What can I possibly do for you?" Howell's hand was shaking as he lifted a small glass of whiskey to his lips.

Knight told him and a surprised Howell whistled between his teeth. "Christ's blood was not in vain," Howell said. "You are a man of complex feelings, aren't you?"

"It's the right thing."

"For you at least, it must be. A heart given to a harlot. Would you like a glass of whiskey?"

"No, but I'd like one bag of gold dust."

"One bag of gold dust," Howell repeated, "and I'm done with you."

The saddlebags of gold were all piled in a corner of his hotel room, and Howell told Knight to help himself. He walked over and lifted a leather flap, reached in and took a fat, canvas pouch and held it awkwardly in his hands.

"I don't like you one bit," Howell said, "but you and deputy Tibbs saved my life. If I'm lucky I'll never see you again. If I'm double lucky I'll hear that you got killed. Besides, I suppose it's my Christian duty to help that woman."

"No offense, Howell, but I've had my fill of people and their Christian duty. I must have read a different Bible."

"You surprise me, marshal, I didn't see you as a man that gave theology any thought."

Knight ignored the insult but his thick fingers squeezed the bag of gold dust. "Let's leave it at that." Nodding politely, he pocketed the gold dust and went out.

Thirty minutes later he found Darla with Dobbs and Tibbs at the Bullhorn Restaurant. He asked if he might join them and Tibbs said they just sat down. They ate together and Darla was tense but obviously pleased to have survived. They were drinking coffee and Knight asked when she was leaving for San Francisco.

"Two Days. That's the next stage, if it's on time."

"This might help you once you get to California," Knight said and palmed the gold dust into her hand. Darla was perplexed.

"What is this?"

Tibbs and Dobbs knew what it was but kept quiet.

"Some gold dust," Knight said softly, "Don't flash it around."

Darla's face scrunched up in disgust, "You don't expect…"

"No, no Darla, I don't, just take it."

Knight pushed his chair back and said, "Good luck, Darla."

He went out before anyone could say anything and he

felt their eyes on him as he left the restaurant. Out on the boardwalk he waited, smoking, knowing that Tibbs and Dobbs would say some things to her, and they would be encouraging. There was a chance anyway, that she'd make it, and that gold might make some things easier. It was all he had to offer, an idea that she might make it.

Tibbs came out first. The sky had darkened and the oil lamps shone through the restaurant window.

"I thought you'd be here."

"Having a smoke."

"Sure. Thought you might like to know I'm going home again to Raven Flats."

"You've got Jamie to look after."

"I'll be working on that. Probably get married. Not sure if I'll remain a lawman."

"You can tell me about it next time."

"Next time. Sure."

"There's money in horses," Knight said. "You might think about that." Knight wanted to make it easy on Tibbs.

"Farming isn't so bad, but I like that idea about horses."

An uncomfortable silence engulfed them. Knight tossed the remnants of his cigarette aside and said, "You'd better get some rest if you're riding home tomorrow. That girl will be happy to see you." They shook hands, and each sensed there was nothing more to say. Tibbs vanished up the boardwalk and Knight wondered if he'd ever see him again.

Knight glanced through the window and Dobbs was getting up. The old wrangler came out, saw Knight and said, "I figured you'd be out here. You see Tibbs?"

"Yup. He's riding home tomorrow."

"Darla's gonna be fine. That was a mighty nice thing you did for her."

"Was it?"

"I'm stickin' around a few days. Drink some, dance a fandango with a woman, eat some beef and potatoes."

"You deserve it. That was a helluva ride. I appreciate all you did."

"Glad I still have my hair."

"See you in Deadwood next time I'm over that way."

"See you, marshal." Dobbs gave Knight a salute by brushing his fingers off the brim of his floppy hat and went on his way. The night had descended on Cheyenne and the town was quiet, a few oil lamps casting sullen glows across the hardpacked street. Knight ambled across the street and walked slowly toward the end of a lane of buildings. It took him a few minutes to find what he was looking for.

The grogshop looked more like a Mexican cantina. Nailed to a board at the door and propped against the stucco wall was a sign that said SMITHY'S. Knight went in and saw two tired looking doves sitting at a plank bar. The barman was a sweating, obese man who examined Knight through slitted eyes.

"You looking for a drink or a woman?" he asked.

"I'd like to speak with a gal named Arlene. Is she around?"

One of the tired looking doves came alive in her chair, standing up and brushing the wrinkles out of her flimsy dress. She smiled and Knight could see in the dim light that she was pretty, but it wouldn't be long before the hard life caught up with her.

"I'm Arlene," she said, still smiling. "Come on back. It's early but we ain't busy."

Before Knight could stop her she spun around and he was forced to follow her down a short hall and into her room. She looked at him expectantly. "It's a dollar," she said.

"I want to explain, Ernie McGruder said to stop over."

Her smile was wider. "That's nice. Ernie's a regular. Glad he recommended the service."

"I'm sorry," Knight said, knowing this was a mistake, but he had come this far and thought he'd better get it done. A man's word is a man's word. "Ernie said that if I got to Cheyenne to tell you he missed you and he'll see you soon."

Her smile never faltered and she opened the lace of her blouse revealing her breasts. "Why, that's real sweet of him."

"The hell of it is, Ernie is dead. He was killed by Indians a few days ago."

Her smile vanished and for a flickering few seconds she looked sad and he thought she might shed a tear. Then her smile returned.

"That's a shame, honey, but don't let that stop you from having a good time. A dollar goes a long way in pleasing a man."

"No, I'm just saying what I promised him." Knight tipped his hat politely. Arlene looked surprised, embarrassment and anger clouding her features.

Her voice clawed after him as he went from the room. "You old fool! Don't come back here unless you have a silver dollar in your hand! You hear me! You ain't nothin' but an old fool!"

Knight paused and turned around. "Yes, ma'am, I've been told that before."

The night breeze carried the sound of a wolf howling in the distance. His fatigue had caught up with him, and he felt empty. For a moment he stood quietly on the boardwalk, lost in the darkness, conscious only of the weight of his holstered Colt on his right hip. He breathed in the cool night air and tried to enjoy the solitude. He tried not to think about anything as he walked to the hotel.

The following morning, after a restless night of turbulent dreams, he bought a new horse and saddle, and when the livery man asked him what name he would give the horse, Knight said, "Vengeance," and the livery man took his money and told him to be on his way. It was a warm, sunflower morning, and the colors were bright except in the west where the sky had darkened. He had a mind to ride up into Montana where he owned a small hunter's cabin near the Bitterroot River, and maybe fish and hunt and get back to reading his old Bible. Maybe. But even as he watched the morning come alive those dark clouds were massing at the horizon like angry spirits. It was an omen, and he believed in omens, but then he thought, I'm a lawman. Better get to it. So he rode west toward a sky the color of blood and knowing that no good would come of it.

THE END

UNDER THE LONESOME SKY
Reader's Discussion Questions

The author appreciates any reviews, blog post discussions or book club discussions or YouTube chat relating to this book!

1: What did you like best about this book?

2: What did you like least about this book?

3: Who would you cast in a film version of this book? Choose any actors living or dead and discuss.

4: Share a favorite quote from the book. Why did this quote stand out?

5: What did you think of the book's length? Was it too long, too short, or just right?

6: The author has stated that his stories are set in the "Mythical West" yet they have a strong background in history. Does this blend of fiction and history work as entertainment for you?

7: What do you think of the book's title? How does the title symbolize the various themes and characterizations? Explain the title in your own words.

8: What do you think of the book's cover? The author chose the cover artwork from his own collection of Western art. How well does it convey what the book is about?

9: What do you think the author's purpose was in writing this book outside of being a Western entertainment? How do the themes, motifs and historical events add texture to the story?

10: How well did the author do in world building the America West in the 1880s?

11: U. S. Marshal Maxfield Knight comes across as a hard, bitter man. Is it possible to feel empathy for him?

12: Although Darla Anderson is a supporting character, she plays a pivotal role at the conclusion. Explain how you feel about Darla, her struggle and her dreams.

13: Is Vincent Two Hatchets a sympathetic character?

14: Explain how Vincent Two Hatchets' actions are understandable yet still horrifying.

15: What does U. S. Marshal Maxfield Knight reveal about himself in his final interaction with Darla.

16: Did the plot and its various twists and turns surprise you in any way?

17: How did the rugged landscape add to the story's suspense?

18: Maxfield Knight's name evokes an image of medieval knights whom are often associated with the ideals of chivalry, a code of noble conduct, and Christian ideologies. How does marshal Knight's conduct fit that image? Do his actions mirror the purported tenets of knighthood or is he the antithesis of knighthood?

19: How memorable was this book?

20: Would you read another book by this author? Why or why not?

ABOUT THE AUTHOR

Thomas McNulty was born in Chicago and is a graduate of the famed writing program at Columbia College. His celebrity interviews, articles, essays, book reviews, film reviews and Hollywood and literary profiles have appeared in numerous magazines including *American Cowboy, Filmfax, The Big Reel, Classic Images, Films of the Golden Age, Kung-Fu Magazine, Mystery News, Scary Monsters* among others. His celebrity interviews included actors and directors Douglas Fairbanks, Jr., Tom Hanks, John Agar, Jackie Chan, Noel Neill, Jack Elam, Burt Kennedy, David Carradine, Jeff Corey, Sheb Wooley, Vincent Sherman, Sam Mendes, Robert Vaughn, and more.

His non-fiction books include the biography *Errol Flynn: The Life and Career* published by McFarland in 2004 and remains in print. Tom's first western adventure novel *Trail of the Burned Man* was followed by many more. One of his best-selling titles is the "New Pulp" novel *The Adventures of Captain Graves* published by Airship 27 Books.

Tom made his screen debut as an extra playing a "bank clerk" in the film *Road to Perdition* (2002), starring Tom Hanks and Paul Newman. He also interviewed and photographed the *Road to Perdition* cast for a series of magazine articles. He was a research contributor to the documentary *The Adventures of Errol Flynn*, for Top Hat Productions for Turner Classic Movies and a contributor to the documentary *Tasmanian Devil: The Fast and Furious Life of Errol Flynn*, for BBC Australia; he provided the audio commentary for the Warner Brothers DVD release of *Rocky Mountain* starring Errol Flynn. Tom can be seen on the TV Land program, *Myths & Legends*, as a guest commentator. Tom's episode is titled, "Curses, Corpses and Alice Cooper."

An avid reader, Tom's other interests include collecting comic books, vintage paperbacks and rare books; target shooting, guitar playing, and fishing. Tom has a Black Belt in Kyuki-Do. He divides his time between Crystal Lake, Illinois and Lac du Flambeau, Wisconsin.

ABOUT THE COVER ARTWORK

Stanley Pitt (1925-2002) was an Australian cartoonist and commercial artist. Pitt was the first Australian comic book artist to have original work published by a major American Comic book company, first with DC's *The Witching Hour*, and subsequently with Western Publishing's Boris Karloff: *Tales of Mystery*. During his lifetime, Pitt acknowledged he was influenced by the classic style of Alex Raymond's artwork for *Flash Gordon*. I acquired this artwork from Cleveland Publishing in Australia who published digest-sized pulp fiction Westerns for over fifty years. Cleveland Publishing was founded in 1953 by Jack Atkins. When Cleveland closed its batwing doors in 2019, I was fortunate to purchase multiple original paintings from their files, including several by Stanley Pitt. His work for Cleveland Westerns was prolific, colorful and charged with emotion and detail. This painting was acquired by Cleveland for use on *Apache Massacre* by Brett Waring. Cleveland's Western fiction legacy and cover artwork are wonderful, and in keeping with the tradition of Western pulp fiction which has inspired my efforts, I am pleased to acknowledge Stanley Pitt's and Cleveland Publishing's contribution by using this image for the book. The original painting is now part of the McNulty Family Western Heritage Collection which includes artwork, rare movie posters, signed books and documents, vintage paperbacks, magazines and comic books.

ABOUT U. S. MARSHAL MAXFIELD KNIGHT

U. S. Marshal Maxfield Knight originated in my short story, *Justice at Ten Sleep Canyon*. This was followed by the short stories *The Ghosts at War Eagle Hill* and *The Outlaw's Dance*, which are included in *Gunfight at Crippled Horse* as bonus stories. These stories were written as part of the natural process of creative writing as I fleshed out the character to see how I felt about him. Maxfield Knight was by now a living, breathing person, and he's here in the room with me now. Knight took over, so to speak, and he appeared in the novel *Showdown at Snakebite Creek* from Robert Hale Publishers in 2011 in England as part of their famed Black Horse Western brand. Maxfield Knight wasn't done with me yet. In 2016 I published another Maxfield Knight adventure, *The Gunsmoke Serenade*, also under the Black Horse Western brand in England. *Ghost Town Gold* was the next U. S. Marshal Maxfield Knight adventure; a novelette where I explored some Western tropes while concentrating on telling a gritty tale. As a book collector, avid reader and baccalaureate holding student of literature, my interests have always been diverse, and my stories often include a dash of the wild pulp fiction plot devices. I am also in the habit of including thematic motifs, allegories and social commentary. As much as I enjoy traditional Westerns, I don't always write simplistic black hat-white hat tales revolving around pursuit and reconciliation. I enjoy delving into the characters in my effort to illuminate what makes them tick. These stories can be read independently of each other as stand-alone novellas. I have several additional Knight stories planned before I conclude his adventures. He is a tough, conflicted buzzard and I suspect his future will be bloody and more than a bit unpleasant. I hope that you'll find him as fascinating to read about as I do in writing about him. Westerns are the quintessential American genre and I am grateful for the opportunity to write these stories. I hope you enjoy them. Max and I will see you again along the dusty trail.

Thomas McNulty
Lac du Flambeau, Wisconsin, August 2023

The U.S. Marshal Maxfield Knight Books
(By publication date)

Showdown at Snakebite Creek (2011)

Gunfight at Crippled Horse (2012, includes three bonus stories)

The Gunsmoke Serenade (2016)

Ghost Town Gold (2019)

Under the Lonesome Sky (2023)

Wounded Outlaw Books –
Remember When Westerns Were Fun?

Remember those thrilling days of yesteryear when Roy and Gene were the star attractions at the Saturday afternoon matinee? Remember when cowboys loved their horses because their horse was their best friend? Remember all those great gunfights, galloping chases, and those wide-open spaces under Western skies? You can experience all of that again with one of Thomas McNulty's fast-action Westerns from Wounded Outlaw Books!

Evoking an era when mass-market pocket Western paperbacks filled spinner racks, these stories are flavored with the gritty, imagistic prose of those grand old pulp Western adventures, and loaded with the charm and heartfelt emotions that comes with a well-told tale. Thomas McNulty's Wounded Outlaw Books brand of stories are diverse and thrilling tales of the Old West and include a wide range of styles: hardboiled thrillers, traditional adventures, and even a tale or two for teenage readers. Saddle up and pick your pleasure!

Produced with professional care and a dash of gunpowder, these books feature blazing cover artwork matched by solid storytelling. The stories are quick, vibrant and tough tales, just the way you like them.

Economically priced, each book is a veritable collector's item. Strap on your gunbelt and ride along with any of these exclusive books by Thomas McNulty and tell your friends – Westerns are fun again!

Printed in the USA
CPSIA information can be obtained
at www.ICGtesting.com
LVHW011356150824
788349LV00005B/519